L in

Dm

RISING TIDE

Separated from her childhood sweetheart Adam, due to a family feud, Grace Brownlow agrees to marry the man chosen for her by her parents. But there are secrets in Thomas's past, as she discovers when she accompanies him back to India. Meanwhile, on his way to India, Adam is hoping to see Grace once more and reassure himself that she is well and happy. But Grace is in trouble. Will Adam arrive in time to help her?

ROBERTA GRIEVE

RISING TIDE

Complete and Unabridged

LINFORD
Leicester

First published in Great Britain in 2012

First Linford Edition
published 2013

A catalogue record for this book is available
from the British Library.

ISBN 978–1–4448–1611–2

Published by
F. A. Thorpe (Publishing)
Anstey, Leicestershire

Set by Words & Graphics Ltd.
Anstey, Leicestershire
Printed and bound in Great Britain by
T. J. International Ltd., Padstow, Cornwall

This book is printed on acid-free paper

1

The tide was in, lapping at the harbour walls. Soon the boats would return, gulls screaming overhead, hovering for the scraps the fishermen would throw overboard.

Grace Brownlow ran along the wall to where it curved its protective arm towards the sea, savouring her first glimpse of the fishing fleet.

She loved these rare moments when she managed to escape from Elsie Manners, her old nurse. Although Grace had long since outgrown the need for a nursemaid, Elsie had stayed with the family as companion and lady's maid and still felt the need to keep a protective eye on her charge.

Grace seized every opportunity to rebel against the restrictions of her life and loved to run free along the waterfront. It was wonderful to feel the wind in her hair, to hear the cries of the seabirds and taste the salt on her lips.

Shading her eyes against the dancing reflections on the water, she watched the boats making their way up the deep water channel towards the harbour entrance, their rust red sails silhouetted against the lowering sun.

Her heart leapt as she spotted the *Emma Jane* — and Adam Crossley. Even from this distance, his shock of jet black hair stood out in stark contrast to the fair heads of the boat's master, Will Smythe and his son Billy.

She couldn't wait for the boat to dock, so determined was she that today she would force a confrontation with Adam — she had to know if he had really meant what he'd said the last time they had been alone together. Her mind thought of that day . . .

★ ★ ★

That evening last summer they had been walking along the foreshore

2

beyond the town and harbour where the salt marshes began. The tide was out, leaving a gleaming expanse of mud, tinged pink by the reflection of the setting sun.

She should have been at home, preparing for bed, but Elsie had fallen asleep in her chair just as she had today. Careful not to wake her, Grace had slipped outside, longing for a breath of fresh air after the heat of the day. She had only intended to walk in the grounds of The Towers but a sudden mischievous impulse had sent her out of the gates and down to the harbour.

The *Emma Jane* had been tied up with the other boats but Adam wasn't there.

Despite being forbidden even to talk to him since he had accused her family of ruining his, she needed to see him, to reassure herself that they were still friends. Surely he didn't include her in his bitterness towards the Brownlows. After all, it wasn't her fault that things had gone wrong.

Frustrated, she'd almost turned for home, but it was a beautiful evening and she carried on walking beyond the harbour and past the boatyards, quiet now that the men had gone home for their evening meal.

Adam had been sitting on a low wall outside one of the cottages that bordered the beach. He had his head in his hands and he looked a picture of despair.

Her heart turned over. Was it his father? Had he taken a turn for the worse? She hesitated and was about to turn away when he looked up and saw her. The smile transformed his face and told her that, whatever the problems between their families, he was still her friend.

He stood up and came towards her, that irrepressible twinkle lighting up his sapphire blue eyes. 'You've managed to escape then?' he said.

'For a while. I ought to be getting back though in case Elsie wakes up.' She hesitated, wanting to ask Adam

4

what was wrong with him but she didn't want to spoil the magic of the moment.

'Walk with me a bit first?'

She nodded and he took her hand. A little thrill went through her and she felt herself blushing. Since she'd last spoken to him he seemed older, more mature. His family's troubles had caused him to grow up fast, she supposed.

They crunched along the pebbly foreshore in silence. Grace didn't want to speak for fear of shattering the wonderful feeling of just being with him. Her heart was beating a little faster than the exercise warranted. Something had changed between them. He was no longer the boy who had taught her to fish, showed her where the best blackberries were to be found.

She stole a glance at him, deciding that she liked the change.

As they reached the salt flats, the lowering sun broke through the cloud and they stood together, hand in hand, watching the changing colours of the sunset reflected in the glistening mud.

As the sky deepened to dark purple, Grace sighed and said, 'I must go home. They'll be missing me.'

'Don't go yet. There's something I must say.' He hesitated and she nodded encouragingly.

He shook his head. 'It's all so complicated. Your family . . . '

'I don't care about them,' she said. 'James has forbidden me to speak to you but it's not up to him. Just because you're poor now doesn't mean you can't be my friend. I really don't understand why James doesn't like you any more.'

She knew she sounded childish but she just wished things could go back to the way they were. It wasn't Adam's fault that his father had lost the business and it wasn't hers that the Brownlows now owned the boatyard that had been in the Crossley family for so long.

'It's nothing to do with being rich or

6

poor,' Adam said. 'It's too complicated to explain.'

He squeezed her hand, pulling her round to face him. 'Grace, I shouldn't — I know I shouldn't — but I must tell you . . . I love you. I've loved you for ages. I promised myself that as soon as you turned sixteen I would ask you . . . ' He broke off, shaking his head. 'Then everything went wrong.'

Grace's heart was pounding. She reached up to touch his face. 'It doesn't matter, Adam. I love you, too, rich or poor.'

He put his arms around her, crushing her to him, and his lips found hers. The kiss was sweet and tender, deepening to passionate intensity. When he released her she gasped. This was what she had dreamed of for so long. She reached for him again but he held her off.

'No, Grace, I shouldn't have. It was wrong of me to encourage you.'

'But, Adam . . . '

'It's no use, my love. Your parents will never allow it. As for my father, you know how he feels about the Brown-lows.'

'There must be a way,' she protested.

'No, my sweet, it would never work.' His expression was sombre. 'I've been thinking of leaving the town, going off to seek my fortune elsewhere. Perhaps I can find work on the colliers, or even join the navy.'

'No, you can't go away!' Grace was horrified. They might be forbidden to meet but at least she could see him often, exchange a glance or a stolen word.

'I can't bear to stay here — seeing you, loving you . . . ' Adam took her hands. 'Just promise you'll never forget me.'

'How could I forget you?'

Grace shook her head, her throat too tight to speak.

He released her hand and fumbled in his pocket, taking out a small box. 'I've got a present for you. It's not much but it's something to remember me by.'

She opened the box, a smile lighting her face as she withdrew the little brooch, a simple oval encrusted with tiny pearls. 'It's beautiful,' she said, pinning it to her collar. 'I shall wear it always.'

'They're real pearls — we find them in mussels sometimes,' Adam told her. 'Ma's been saving them for years. I got the jeweller in the High Street to set them for me.' He helped her to pin the brooch to her shawl. 'Maybe one day I'll be able to buy you real jewels — diamonds and emeralds . . . '

'This means far more to me,' Grace said. She leaned forward, kissing his cheek and hoping he would pull her into his arms again.

But he pushed her gently away and said, 'You must go home before they send out a search party.'

He had walked her back to the gates of The Towers and waited until she was inside.

★ ★ ★

Since then she had tried many times to see him but her parents, as well as her brother, seemed to sense that she was on the verge of rebellion and kept a tighter rein on her.

She didn't understand why James hated Adam so much. Some of her happiest memories were of being allowed to play with the two boys. Now, they were sworn enemies.

'I don't want you hobnobbing with the fishermen,' James had told her more than once. She knew it was just a way of keeping her and Adam apart.

She didn't care that his family were poor, that he now had to earn a living on the fishing boats. She didn't care either that she'd been forbidden to have anything to do with him since their families had become estranged. If James knew how often she came down to the harbour — and especially if he knew why she came — he'd be furious.

Grace knew that Adam blamed the Brownlows for the tragedy that had left his family without a breadwinner.

Adam's mother now had to take in washing and he did any work that was available to help support his family.

But it was hardly her fault, she thought, remembering the accident which had crippled Abel Crossley.

The friendship between the two families had already begun to cool before Abel had lost his leg. Grace had been too young to understand, although she knew it had something to do with business. When, as a result of the accident, the Crossleys lost their boatyard and house, Adam had accused Grace's family.

It was true her father had taken over the boatyard together with its debts, but, as he'd explained to her, it was to help his old friend. Adam didn't see it like that and his bitterness had grown with the passing years.

Nevertheless, Grace simply couldn't help how she felt about Adam — and he felt the same, she knew now that he did.

As the boats lowered their sails and

eased their way through the harbour entrance, she tried to will Adam to look up and smile — or would he avoid her as he had done ever since that evening last summer?

Today, knowing that her father and brother were down at the boatyard and her mother engaged in her charity work, she had once more managed to give Elsie the slip and hurried down to the harbour. She must speak to him before he made good his threat to leave the town and seek work elsewhere.

Surely if they loved each other, they could overcome the objections of their families, she thought, fingering the little brooch which, true to her promise, she wore every day.

Although, deep down, she admitted that Adam was right, given the hatred the older generation of Crossleys and Brownlows had for each other, she felt she must see him one last time, before it was too late.

Grace bit her lip, knowing she should turn away, go home to the big house up on the hill with its luxurious furnishings and its servants before she was missed. There were strict rules for a well-brought-up young lady and they did not include running wild along the harbour and waterfront, chatting to the boat-builders and fishermen as she had when she was a child.

But she couldn't go home without trying to speak to Adam, especially now that she had a good idea of what awaited her back at The Towers. Her mother had been in a state all day over their dinner guest and Grace knew that she had another suitor lined up for her.

How long would it be before she gave in to the pressure to conform to her parents' wishes? No, she thought, she'd defy them as she had so often before. Loving Adam as she did, she couldn't marry someone else — but would he have the courage to defy convention too?

The boats were in and she took a step forward, lifting her hand to wave. Her foot caught a pile of oyster shells and she tripped. Her feet skidded on the slippery harbour wall and she plunged into the icy water, gasping as it closed over her head.

She opened her mouth to scream, coughing as her mouth filled with sea water. Her chest burned and she struggled to fight her way to the surface. Panicking, she kicked out, but her heavy skirts and layers of petticoats were pulling her down. It was no use, she thought as she fought to breath. Her eyes closed and she almost gave up the struggle but, as she began to lose consciousness, she felt something tugging at her hair. She'd become caught up in something. Panic engulfed her once more and she lashed out.

Someone grabbed her arms and she was dimly aware of a voice in her ear. 'Don't struggle. I'll have you out in a jiffy.'

Barely conscious now, she felt herself being lifted up and laid on the rough ground. She began to cough and sea water poured from her mouth. Then she fainted.

★　★　★

Adam looked up from sorting the fish and grinned at his mate. 'Good catch today, Billy,' he said with a grin.

'Best for a long time,' Billy Smythe replied.

It was about time their luck changed, Adam thought. The fishing hadn't been good lately, scarce enough to warrant putting it on the train for Billingsgate where it would fetch a better price than locally. Adam counted himself fortunate to have been taken on the *Emma Jane* which was owned by Billy's father. Will Smythe always made sure Adam received a fair share of the haul, however poor the catch might have been. It was enough to keep his family from the workhouse anyway.

A spasm of anger crossed Adam's face at the thought. If it wasn't for the Brownlows . . .

The *Emma Jane* was nosing its way into the harbour, vying for space with the Sea Sprite and Will shouted at the lads to help furl the sails, before grabbing the ropes to tie her up to the harbour wall.

As Adam hurried to obey he heard a cry and a splash. He ran to the side and looked over into the deep waters of the harbour. 'It's just someone dumping rubbish overboard,' Will shouted. 'Get those sails down.'

But as Adam turned away, he spotted a flash of emerald green silk. That wasn't rubbish — and hadn't he heard someone cry out? Will was still shouting at him but he ignored the boat's master and leaned over the side again. This time he saw a small white arm, a hand feebly clutching at the air. Without thinking he threw off his oilskin coat, leapt up on the rail and dived into the murky depths.

He came up coughing, shaking his head to clear the water from his eyes. There was no sign of anyone. He dived down again, peering through the murky water. He reached out, grabbing a handful of hair and hands flailed at him. He managed to get his arms around the body and swam strongly towards the steps. Gasping for breath, he heaved his burden onto the slippery seaweed covered steps. It was heavy, weighed down by the waterlogged material in the voluminous skirts.

Willing hands reached out to help him out of the water. They laid the girl on the harbour wall and Adam looked more closely at her. The skin around her lips was blue but she was still breathing. He squatted down and brushed the tangled strands of golden hair from her face, gasping as he recognised her. What had she been doing walking along the harbour wall alone?

'Oh, god, Grace! Speak to me, please . . . ' He grabbed her hands, rubbing them between his own to try and instil some warmth into them. His heart was pounding. Would she live? He couldn't bear it if . . .

He choked back a sob as all the love he'd tried so hard to suppress welled up in him. Dear, sweet Gracie, his companion of childhood days, was lost to him now, even if she survived. No, she couldn't be. There must be a way. He had spoken bravely about going off to seek his fortune but here he was, still working at the fishing. Would Grace be content in a lowly fisherman's cottage? She would say yes, he knew that, but he couldn't ask it of her.

He released her hands and stroked her face and hair, willing her to open her eyes, his lips moving in silent prayer.

Suddenly a violent tremor shook her and she gasped, a rush of sea water gushing from her mouth.

'Gracie, my sweet! You're all right. Thank God.'

Her eyelids fluttered and she smiled up at him. 'Adam,' she whispered, then her eyes closed and she lost consciousness once more.

18

He shrugged off his oilskin coat and tenderly laid it over her, only to see it snatched away. 'Take your hands off my sister,' a voice snarled.

He looked up to see James Brownlow standing over him. A crowd had gathered on the harbour wall, fishermen whose boats now thronged the harbour leaned over the side to see what all the fuss was about.

Adam looked around at them, bewildered. 'I was only trying to . . . ' he stuttered.

James Brownlow glared at him. 'Leave her alone,' he snapped, gathering his sister up in his arms. Hands reached out to help but he brushed them aside.

Will Smythe was not to be deterred. He planted himself in front of the young man. 'No call to be like that, Mr James,' he said firmly. 'If it wasn't for young Adam here, your sister would've drowned.'

James ignored him and stalked towards his pony and trap, cradling Grace in his arms. Adam watched silently, praying that she would be all right. Will clapped him on the shoulder. 'Well done, lad,' he said. 'Good job you spotted her — not that you'll get any thanks from the likes of that lot.'

Adam didn't want thanks, he was just grateful that he'd been there, that it seemed he had got her out of the water in time. Her brother would see that she was cared for. Whatever his personal feelings about James Brownlow, he knew that he loved his sister and would look after her.

He shuddered, recalling the way James had looked at him when he realised who it was that had pulled Grace from the water. Hard to believe, from the hatred in his eyes, that they had once been friends.

2

Grace became aware of the jolting and swaying of the trap, the steady clip-clop of the pony's hooves on the road. Strong arms held her and she sighed. 'Adam,' she murmured. 'You saved me . . . '

A cynical laugh jolted her into full awareness and she opened her eyes, looking up into the grim face of her brother. 'Still mooning over that fisher lad?' he sneered.

Grace struggled to sit up and her eyes blazed. 'He pulled me out of the water. I could've drowned.'

'If you hadn't been down at the harbour in the first place you wouldn't have fallen in. I don't know what Mother will say when she hears what you've been up to.'

She struggled to sit up, shivering in her wet clothes. 'You won't tell her, will you? Please, James.'

'She'll know something's happened when she sees the state of you,' James said. 'Don't worry, I'll say you were with me. It's a good job I followed you and got there in time.'

He made it sound as if he was the one who had rescued her. When they reached home he would probably embroider the tale, make himself out to be a hero.

Grace knew she'd have to play along with him if she wanted to be spared her parents' anger. That was the price of his silence about her escapade. Anything to try and impress their father, she thought. And who would dare to call him a liar?

The fishermen rarely came in contact with the Brownlows these days. As for the men who worked for them in the shipyard, who would surely hear the story in the taverns and public houses that evening, they would be too frightened of their employer to dare to speak up.

She closed her eyes and a small smile played at the corners of her mouth as she recalled Adam's tender gestures. In those moments before she had fainted again she had seen the look in his eyes and she knew that, however much he tried to hide it, he still loved her. She hugged the knowledge to her, determined now to resist her parents' efforts to marry her off to what they considered a suitable man.

As the pony slowed in front of the house, a groom hurried forward to take the reins. 'Is Miss Grace all right?' he asked, noting her pallor and tangled wet hair.

She struggled upright and smiled at the lad. 'A little accident. Nothing to worry about,' she said before James could reply.

James helped her down from the trap. 'Better get inside and out of those wet things. I'll tell Father what happened — not the whole story of course.' He smiled, a cruel baring of the lips, no warmth in it. 'And don't worry, your secret is safe with me.'

Grace glared at him. 'Don't feel you have to lie on my behalf,' she snapped, colour returning to her cheeks.

He grinned again. 'Anything for you, sis,' he said.

Elsie Manners rushed towards them as they entered the house, exclaiming over Grace's dishevelled state.

'Don't fuss, Elsie. Just help me get changed before Mother sees me,' she said.

Upstairs in her room, she shrugged out of her wet clothes and wrapped herself in a warm robe. Elsie began to brush the tangles and strands of seaweed out of her hair, her lips compressed in a tight line as she tried to contain her curiosity.

Grace, now completely recovered from her ordeal, smiled at her in the mirror and told her, 'I fell in the harbour — slipped on a patch of seaweed.'

'Oh, Miss Grace, what were you doing down by the water? You know the master has forbidden it unless you're with Mister James or one of the grooms.'

Elsie had been with the family a long time and Grace knew she was fond of her so she forgave the familiarity. 'I was with my brother,' she said, blushing slightly at the lie. 'You saw him bring me home.'

'I also saw you creeping out of the side door and running across the slopes to the beach path,' Elsie said. She paused and waved the hairbrush for emphasis. 'Why do you do it, Miss Grace? You know you'll get caught out one day.'

'I don't know,' Grace admitted. 'It's just ... being stuck in this house, having to act ladylike all the time. I can't get used to it. I just wish things would go back to how they were when I was little, before we got rich and came to live here.'

'Most young girls would give anything to have the advantages you have,' Elsie said. 'Beautiful dresses, parties, handsome young men dancing attendance . . . '

'I don't care about all that,' Grace said, her lips set in a petulant frown.

Elsie brushed out the last tangles and began to pin Grace's hair up in a smooth chignon. She helped her into fresh clothes, lacing the bodice tightly to show off the girl's burgeoning figure, and fastening a string of pearls around her slim neck.

'I don't see why I have to dress up for dinner every day,' Grace protested.

'It's the done thing. Besides, have you forgotten your parents are entertaining tonight?'

Grace had not forgotten and she sighed.

She had lost count of the number of suitors, young and old, who had been paraded in front of her since her sixteenth birthday. Her mother had said she was free to choose for herself, as long as the man of her choice was from the right background — and rich.

She sighed. If she could really

choose, she knew there was only one man for her. And if she couldn't have Adam, she would remain a spinster rather than marry a man she did not love, especially for money. Weren't her family rich enough already?

★ ★ ★

Grace made her way down the wide staircase to the panelled hall where a number of guests stood around chatting with glasses in their hands.

Her mother swept towards her. 'Oh, there you are, my dear. Now we can go in to dinner.'

She turned and spoke to the young man behind her. 'Allow me to introduce my daughter. Grace, this is Thomas Eastwood. He has just returned from India.'

The young man smiled and took Grace's hand. 'Charmed, Miss Brownlow,' he said.

'Pleased to meet you, Mr Eastwood,' Grace replied. She kept her own smile firmly in place but her heart sank. Her mother would have arranged for her to be seated next to him at dinner and she would have to make polite small talk all evening, pretending an interest in him and whatever his business in India might have been.

The meal seemed to go on forever, course after course of elaborate dishes — oysters in a rich sauce that masked the fresh salty flavour of the simple seafood Grace had enjoyed in happier days; syllabubs and trifles suffused with alcohol that gave her a headache. She began to feel a little sick, partly as the result of having swallowed so much sea water earlier on, and she longed to leave the table. But her mother knew nothing of her narrow escape — James had kept his promise not to tell in return for her own assurance that she would keep away from the harbour in future. Under Mother's stern gaze she had to pretend to be enjoying both the meal and the company.

Thomas Eastwood was a pleasant enough young man, well mannered and good looking. He had dark brown eyes and sleek black hair. His teeth gleamed white in his tanned face, the result of living so long in India she supposed.

But he wasn't Adam. She smiled and nodded in reply to one of his comments but her thoughts were far away.

She knew she wouldn't be able to keep her promise to James. She would have to escape from the house somehow and go down to the harbour. She hadn't had the chance to speak to him today but she must know if there was any chance of a future for them. Besides, she hadn't thanked him for risking his own life to save her.

If he pushed her away this time, she would try to put him out of her heart and mind and become the dutiful daughter her parents demanded.

Perhaps she should start now, she thought, turning to Thomas and smiling. 'Tell me more, Mr Eastwood. It sounds fascinating,' she said.

He didn't need further encouragement. 'India is a wonderful country, Miss Grace. So many opportunities for young men.'

'But you have come back to England to live?'

'I've made my fortune and I had a longing to settle back here in the old country.' He went on to tell her how he'd been sent to school in England at a very young age. 'It was too long a journey to go home in the holidays so I travelled around the country staying with various friends and relatives.'

'And what made you decide to settle here?' Grace was doing her best to sound interested.

'My father wanted me to join him in Scotland when he retired, but sadly he died. I didn't want to stay there — it was too bleak for me. I'd visited Kent some years ago and fell in love with the countryside. Much as I love India, the climate is not conducive to good health — there are the monsoons, when it rains incessantly for weeks on end.'

'It sounds very interesting though,' she said. 'I have read of India, of course.'

'Books are no substitute for the real thing,' he said smiling.

'But you won't go back? You will be settling permanently in our little town?' Grace asked.

'I may have to return soon — a matter of business — but I intend to spend the rest of my days here,' he said.

When he went on to tell her of his plans for buying a house in a nearby village and about the yacht her father was building for him, she lost interest. Talking about a far off exotic country had served to take her mind off Adam, but only for a few moments. Speaking of boats being built reminded her of Adam's situation and the impossibility of her family and his ever agreeing to a match between them. And, despite knowing that Adam truly loved her, she was beginning to wonder if he could ever forget that she was the daughter of the man who had ruined his family.

31

Could their love surmount the bitterness and enmity he felt towards her father?

* * *

Adam, shivering in his wet clothes, gazed after the pony and trap long after it was out of sight, praying that Grace would suffer no lasting effects from her near drowning. Not that anyone from the Brownlow household would be likely to pass on any news of her, he thought. With a resigned shrug, he jumped back on board the *Emma Jane*, prepared to help with unloading the catch despite the chill in his body.

But as he bent to pick up a box of fish, Will Smythe handed him his oilskin coat, saying. 'Get on home lad. Don't want you catching a chill. I'll need you on the boat tomorrow.'

Gratefully, Adam shrugged the coat on over his wet clothes, his teeth chattering now. 'Don't worry, Mr Smythe, I'll be here bright and early.'

He would too — he couldn't afford even one day away from work.

Will nodded. 'I know you will, lad.'

The heavy coat did nothing to warm him, the wet jersey underneath clinging to his chilled body as he hurried through the narrow streets behind the harbour.

Inside the cottage his father was sitting at the kitchen table and his mother stood at the cast iron range stirring something in a big pot. She turned, gasping at his pale face and trembling hands. Sarah Crossley was used to her son coming home in wet clothes, exhausted from battling the waves out in the North Sea, but she could see something far worse had happened today.

'What is it, son?' she said, hurrying towards him and helping him off with his coat, exclaiming over the sodden jersey beneath.

'It's all right, Ma,' he said. 'No harm done. It's not the first time I've fallen in.' He was reluctant to tell his parents what had happened. Any mention of the Brownlows was guaranteed to get his father ranting about the wrongs they had done him. It had all happened years ago but he couldn't let it go.

Adam just didn't feel up to hearing it all again, knowing that this time he might not be able to hide his true feelings. He understood his father's bitterness and sympathised, up to a point, but he felt it was time Dad put it behind him and got on with his life. After all, there were plenty of men who'd been crippled by accidents at sea and in the boatyards and they still managed to earn a living and provide for their families. He felt sure Will Smythe would have found work for him, either sorting the fish on the quayside or mending nets or sails. They weren't the sort of jobs you needed two legs for.

Adam hated seeing his mother working so hard at doing other people's laundry while Dad sat at home bewailing his lot and cursing the Brownlows.

While his mother fussed round him, fetching warm towels from the line strung in front of the fire and gathering up the clothes he had shed, he told her that he'd slipped when jumping off the boat.

He could tell his mother didn't believe him and she was sure to hear the true story sooner or later — gossip travelled fast in the small harbour town.

Hopefully, she wouldn't mention it to Dad.

With dry clothes and a bowl of stew inside him his face began to regain its normal ruddy colour and the trembling stopped. He still felt cold though and he got up to sit in front of the range.

'You should be more careful, son,' his father said.

'Leave him be, Abel,' said Sarah. 'I don't suppose he fell overboard on purpose.'

Adam felt his face reddening and hoped she would attribute it to the heat from the fire. He had jumped into the sea without thinking, not realising who had fallen in. He'd have done the same for anyone. It was just coincidence that it had been Grace and that he'd been there to save her.

He closed his eyes, suddenly exhausted, but the image of Grace wouldn't go away. He found himself thinking back to their childhood when the families had been friends, before old Josiah Brownlow had made a fortune and built his house up on the slopes above the town; before he'd started lording it over the lesser folk and taught his son and grandson to do the same.

The Crossleys had been prosperous enough in those days too, Adam's grandfather, Noah, making a good living from boat-building. Back then the family had lived in a neat brick-built villa set back behind the boatyard which took up a fair section of the foreshore. Grace's grandfather, Josiah, was a boat-builder too in those days, his yard and workshops alongside the Crossleys'.

It was the building of the harbour that changed everything — that and the coming of the railway. It had brought prosperity to the small town — for some at least.

Josiah had invested in the harbour and begun importing wood for his boats from Scandinavia. He had orders from rich gentlefolk who were becoming interested in sailing for sport and leisure. Adam's grandfather had preferred to stick with the more traditional oyster yawls and barges that his business had been founded on. There was room for both of them and, for a time, both businesses flourished.

Others in the town weren't so fortunate. For several years the fishing was poor, and then the oyster harvest which so many depended on failed, the stocks depleted by a mystery disease. Destitute families queued at the soup kitchens set up by the more affluent inhabitants, among them Noah Crossley.

But not Josiah Brownlow. He didn't

see why his hard-earned money should go to help those he thought of as too idle to go and seek work. He and Noah often argued but they did not fall out over it. That came later.

Adam had heard the story so many times. Relations between the two families had cooled a little, but not enough to stop the children playing together. He still treasured happy memories of playing on the foreshore with James and Grace, wandering up on the Downs behind the town to pick blackberries and chestnuts.

Then it had all changed.

He'd always loved helping down at the boatyard and he'd been looking forward to leaving school and becoming apprenticed to his father. He remembered coming home from school that day, sitting up at the table to eat the meal his mother had placed in front of him.

'Dad's still at the yard,' she said. 'Eat up and you can go and give him a hand, but don't let him stay too late

— he works too hard.'

Adam knew things had not been going well with the business and he was relieved that his father was confident enough of things improving that he was prepared to take him on.

He had finished his meal quickly and dashed across the road. The sight that met him still played on his mind even all these years later . . . He had heard voices arguing, seen Charles Brownlow stomping out of the workshop. Then came the sound of falling wood.

Dad was almost buried beneath a heap of timber, groaning in pain as Adam tried to lift the heavy planks. Then James Brownlow appeared out of nowhere to offer his help. He could still see his mother's stricken face, hear her loud wails when she heard that her husband lay dying in the hospital up on the hill. They had rushed to the hospital, dreading what they would find. It seemed hours before the doctor came out and told them what had happened.

'He'll be all right, won't he?' Sarah asked, her hand pressed to her lips as he shook his head.

'Too soon to tell, Mrs Crossley. He has massive injuries. It's fortunate your son came along when he did. We've done our best to make him comfortable.'

'Can we see him?'

'Best to let him rest for now. Come back in the morning. We'll have more news then.' He patted her arm sympathetically and turned to Adam. 'Look after your mother, son. She's going to need you now,' he said.

Sarah began to sob and Adam led her away.

When they got back to the cottage, one of the carpenters from the boat yard was there.

'Is he . . . ?' He twisted his cap between his fingers.

Adam shook his head. 'He's still alive but we don't know . . . '

'What happened, Jim? Were you there?' Sarah asked.

'We'd all knocked off for the day but Mr Crossley stayed behind. I went back for my bait tin and saw Adam and young Mr James trying to lift the wood off him. I went for help and luckily Mr Brownlow was just leaving his own yard so I called him over. When we got him out he took the boss up to the hospital in his pony and trap.'

Sarah thanked him and the man left, promising to try and keep things going while the boss was laid up. He didn't express the thought that was in all their minds — that Abel Crossley might not live through the night.

* * *

Abel had survived but his injuries kept him in the hospital for many weeks. Adam never went back to school but he didn't become an apprentice either. He'd gone down to the boatyard but there was little he could do. Without his father, the men became idle, griping about not getting their wages.

41

With no money coming in, Sarah started to take in washing and Adam had turned the mangle for her and helped fold the sheets, then delivered them to the big houses. He'd run errands to earn a few coppers and gone down to the harbour to watch the boats come in, offering to sort the fish.

Until the accident it had never occurred to him to think about money or the lack of it. His father's boat-building business, while not making them rich, had brought a comfortable living and his mother hadn't had to work.

Suddenly everything had changed. One evening he'd returned home from an errand to see his mother sitting by the fire, her head in her hands, sobbing.

For a moment his heart had lurched. Was Father dead? Hadn't everyone said he was getting better? Tentatively, he laid a hand on his mother's arm and she looked up at him, her face full of emotion and streaked with tears. She pulled him towards her and hugged him tight.

His voice trembled as he asked, 'Is it Dad?'

'No, no — he's on the mend — he'll be home soon,' she reassured him.

'What's wrong then?' There was new maturity in his voice. He'd had to grow up fast in the last two months.

'I don't know how we're going to manage. There's no money. The business . . . ' Her voice faltered.

Adam didn't understand. At the time of the accident, Abel Crossley had been putting the finishing touches to an oyster yawl and there was another boat already started. The last time he'd been down to the boatyard he'd been pleased to see the men his father employed hard at work. Perhaps they'd realised that things would surely pick up when they were paid for the finished boats and they would get their wages. Ma could also stop doing other people's washing and everything would be how it was before the accident.

'Don't cry, Ma.' He felt so helpless watching her struggling to get control of her tears.

She wiped her eyes on her apron. 'You'll have to know some time, son. The boatyard doesn't belong to us any more.' Her voice broke and she took a deep breath before continuing. 'The wood hasn't been paid for and the suppliers were threatening us with the bailiffs. They refused to wait till the boat was finished, said there'd already been too much delay.'

'But the yawl for Mr Gann is almost finished. I saw the men working on it yesterday. He'll pay up any day now and then we can pay for the wood.' Young as he was, Adam had a good head for business, having watched his father poring over the books every evening after work.

Sarah Crossley gave a bitter half laugh. 'It's Charles Brownlow will be getting the money for that yawl,' she said.

'Mr Brownlow? I don't understand.'

'He's the owner of the yard now. He's taken over your father's debts. Mr Gann didn't want to wait for his boat — work had stopped in the yard since Dad's accident and no one was getting paid, so the men were looking for other work. Charles stepped in . . . '

Her voice broke on a sob and she drew Adam to her, hugging him fiercely. 'Oh, son, we thought your father was going to die and it seemed the only way out — our debts paid and money to pay for doctors . . . '

Adam felt tears welling up and his throat closed, but he wouldn't cry. Ma needed him now. He would truly have to be the man of the house — that is, until Dad was well enough to work again. They had the house, bought and paid for. Adam was already learning the rudiments of boat building. They could start over and build a business again.

But by the time his father was well enough to come home, it wasn't to the house Adam had lived in all his life. That had been sold to pay their mounting debts and he and his mother had moved to a tiny weather-boarded cottage in an alley just off the High Street. There was no running water, and a privy at the end of the yard.

'Thank goodness your grandfather isn't alive to see what we've come to, although if he was it would never have happened,' Sarah said, looking round the tiny kitchen. 'I don't know how Charles could have done this to your father. Your grandad and Josiah had their differences but at heart they were true friends.' Her lips thinned. 'But Josiah's son — he's a different breed — selfish, greedy.'

Adam was shocked at the venom in is mother's voice. This was Grace's father they were talking about. He knew that Charles Brownlow was spoken of in town as a hard-headed businessman but he'd always thought he was a fair man. 'We won't always be poor though. When Dad gets back to work . . . '

'That's not going to happen, son. Your father won't be able to work — at least not for a long time. I should have told you before but I hoped . . . ' She choked back a sob. 'He got an infection — they had to take his leg off. He's taken it hard — not just his leg, but losing his livelihood too.'

She sank into a chair and covered her face with her hands. 'What's going to become of us?'

Adam stood for a moment, shock leaving him unable to offer words of comfort as he tried to imagine his father — that strong, hard-working man — with only one leg, a cripple.

He straightened his shoulders. 'Don't worry, Ma. I'll look after you — and Dad. Perhaps I could work for Mr Brownlow until I've paid off the debt.'

Sarah shook her head. 'Your father wouldn't hear of it. He hates the Brownlows now.'

3

Grace gazed out of the window across the green slopes towards the sea, her needlework idle in her lap. Far away on the horizon she could see the returning fishing fleet. The short winter day was drawing to a close and, from this distance, silhouetted against the setting sun, the sails looked black, instead of rich russet red. If only she could run down to the harbour and watch the boats coming in and unloading their catch . . . but she hadn't been allowed out by herself since falling in the water all those weeks ago.

Elizabeth Brownlow's voice interrupted her thoughts 'Daydreaming again? You haven't heard a word I said.'

Grace looked round, a faint flush stealing across her cheeks. 'I'm sorry, Mother. What did you say?'

'I was asking what you thought of Mr

Eastwood. He is a well set up young man, is he not?'

'He seems very pleasant, Mother,' Grace replied.

'He comes from a very good family.'

Grace could not care less if he were rich or poor, ugly or handsome. He could never match up to Adam Crossley in her eyes. She forced a smile and feigned interest. No one, least of all her parents, must ever suspect how she felt about Adam.

James had kept his promise not to tell their parents of her mishap, letting them think that he'd rescued her himself. Grace had kept quiet, anxious to avoid a row. Her brother enjoyed being thought a hero while she was just relieved that Adam's name had not been mentioned.

Her mother was still talking about Thomas Eastwood. 'He seems very taken with you, my dear,' she said. 'You could do worse. You must make yourself agreeable to him when he dines with us again this evening.'

'Must I, Mother?' Grace couldn't help herself. Pleasant as Thomas Eastwood had seemed at their first meeting, she couldn't think of him in that way. And it wasn't just because her heart already belonged to Adam.

Her mother replied sharply. 'Yes, you must, Grace. It's time you started thinking of courtship and marriage. Many girls your age are already spoken for, and it would be a good match.'

'But, Mother. I don't want to think of marriage yet.' *Least of all to Thomas Eastwood,* she added silently to herself. Now, if they were talking about Adam ... She felt herself blushing and her mother smiled.

'Such an innocent,' she said fondly, completely misinterpreting the cause of Grace's reddened cheeks. 'But that's as it should be.' Elizabeth put down her needlework and sighed. 'You're quite old enough, Grace. It would be an excellent match, and besides, you'll be lucky to meet anyone more suitable in this town.'

Her tone told Grace quite plainly how her mother felt about her husband's home town. She had no love for the narrow rambling streets with their weather-boarded cottages and the foreshore with its noisy, smelly boat-building and fishing industries. Despite these very industries being the source of her husband's wealth, she felt herself too good for the common townsfolk. When her father-in-law had built his mansion on the slopes to the east of the town, she had been unable to hide her delight that the Brownlows had gone up in the world and had jumped at the chance to move into The Towers.

Elizabeth had been brought up in a large Georgian townhouse in one of London's select squares and had met her husband though her father's business interests. Her knowledge of seaside towns had been coloured by summer visits to Eastbourne where posh hotels fronted the promenade and fashionable ladies paraded their finery on the pier.

Coming to this little town on the north Kent coast had been something of a shock and it had taken her some time to settle. Moving from their more humble home on the waterfront to The Towers had cheered her up, especially when she'd been able to start mixing with what passed for the gentry around here.

Grace knew that her mother was ambitious for her and, for a girl of her station in life, a good marriage was the only way to move up the social ladder. Before she could say anything else, the maid came in with their afternoon tea. She put the heavy tray down on the side table and went across to draw the heavy brocade curtains across, shutting out the gathering twilight and Grace's view of the sea.

After making up the fire, she left the room and Grace offered to pour the tea. Handing the fine bone china cup and saucer to her mother gave her the opportunity to change the subject.

'We'll miss James when he goes to

London,' she said. It wasn't really true. Since her fall into the harbour, her relationship with her brother had changed. It was sometimes hard to reconcile the hard-faced man he had become with the boy who had once been her playmate. He was getting more like their father every day — only concerned with making money and with his standing in the town — and now he was going to manage the office their father had opened in London and was full of self-importance at the responsibility he'd been given.

In a way, she was glad he was going. One less person to watch and criticise her every move, she thought.

'Young men must spread their wings,' Elizabeth said, taking a dainty sip from her tea. 'And it will be an excellent opportunity for him to meet the right sort of people.'

'I wish I could go with him,' Grace said, without thinking. She felt it unfair that being a girl she was not allowed a say in the business. She felt she had just as much right as her brother to be involved.

'Nonsense, Grace. Your brother will be staying in lodgings — no place for a young girl on her own. Now, if we had a house in town, we could spend time there, go to the theatre and meet the right sort of people.' Elizabeth sighed. 'Well, we don't have to worry about your future now. You will have a fine house and you've been taught the necessary skills for a young lady of breeding. You can do fine needlework and play the piano. You will be able to manage a home and will make an excellent hostess for your future husband.'

They were back to that again, Grace thought, with a sigh. It seemed that Mother had decided on her future — and that future would be with Thomas Eastwood.

Not if I have anything to do with it, she told herself. She would make herself as disagreeable to the young man as she possibly could — without raising her mother's suspicions, of course.

Thomas had been a frequent visitor to The Towers since that autumn day when she'd fallen in the harbour and with each meeting she had come to dread seeing him again, for despite his ready smile and easy manner, there was a coldness about him that chilled her. That smile never seemed to really reach his eyes, as if he were making a deliberate effort to be agreeable.

It wasn't just that she was already in love; even if she'd never met Adam, she would have been loath to give Thomas Eastwood any encouragement. But how could she explain this to her parents, who only saw a personable young man who'd made his fortune abroad and come home to seek a suitable wife — in their eyes an excellent match for their only daughter?

Grace helped herself to a slice of fruit cake although she wasn't really hungry, but if she refused to eat her mother would think there was something wrong with her and she did hate a fuss. Looking at the dainty sandwiches, the scones and cakes piled high on the small table — enough for a large family rather than two people — she thought about Mrs Crossley, struggling to feed her husband and son on the small amount that Adam earned on the *Emma Jane*.

The small mouthful of cake nearly choked her as she thought back to those happy days before the Crossleys' business had started to falter, made worse by Abel Crossley's accident. That was when the friendship between the two families had turned to enmity. Grace wondered, as she often had, what had happened to change things. It wasn't just that Adam's family was now poor, while the Brownlows had gone up in the world and begun to think themselves too good for their former friends.

As for Adam, she sometimes wondered why he bothered to speak to her at all when it was obvious he had come to hate her family — but that petulant thought didn't last long as she recalled the despair in his voice when he had thought she was drowned and the tenderness of his touch as she regained consciousness.

They had almost finished tea when her father came in, rubbing his hands and smiling. 'Another order in the bag,' he announced, turning to James who had followed him into the room. 'You're getting good at clinching deals, son. Perhaps you should stay and work with me, rather than go off to London.'

Before he could reply, Elizabeth spoke up. 'Don't talk nonsense, Charles. Of course he must go. Now, sit down and have tea and let's have no more business talk. This is not the place for it.'

Grace stood and dutifully poured tea for her father and brother, then handed round the sandwiches.

James filled his plate and began to eat hungrily. 'The sea air gives you an appetite,' he mumbled through a mouthful of food when Elizabeth remonstrated with him.

'Nevertheless, remember your manners,' she said.

'Oh, leave the lad alone,' Charles said, turning to his daughter. 'And what have you been up to today?' he asked.

'Nothing much,' she said, showing him her embroidery. He barely glanced at it, and in an effort to engage his interest she asked, 'Are you going to build another sloop? Who for?'

Before he could reply, Elizabeth said, 'Grace, that doesn't concern you. Let the men talk their business in the office or down at the yard.'

'I'm interested, that's all,' she said.

Elizabeth sighed. 'I knew no good would come of letting you go down to the foreshore so often when you were small. I don't see what's so fascinating about watching men sawing wood and forging iron.'

'It's what pays for your fine silks and laces, my dear,' Charles said mildly.

Elizabeth sighed heavily and, replacing her cup and saucer on the tray, she picked up the hand bell to summon the maid. When the girl had taken the tea things away, she turned to her husband. 'I have something far more important to talk about — your daughter's future,' she said.

Grace sat up straight. 'What do you mean, Mother?' she asked, although she had a good idea what was to follow.

Elizabeth ignored her. 'Charles, this is important. You told me Mr Eastwood was interested in Grace. Has he said any more on the subject?'

'Not directly, but he is coming to dinner again tonight. He knows he has my blessing. He will probably declare himself if he is given an opportunity to be alone with Grace. I suggest we give him that opportunity.'

'But, Father . . . ' Grace protested.

'What's the matter, child? You find Mr Eastwood quite agreeable, don't you?'

'I suppose so, but I hardly know him.'

It was a poor excuse. She had been given ample opportunity to talk to him while her parents conversed with their other guests and he had told her a little about his adventures in India.

As far as her parents were concerned that was quite adequate, but Grace wondered how she could possibly base a life-long marriage on such a meagre acquaintance.

★ ★ ★

Seated beside Thomas at dinner that evening, Grace couldn't help agreeing that it all sounded very exciting as he extolled the beauties of that far off land — the exotic plants and animals, the vibrant colours of the native women's dress, the noisy bazaars filling the air with a fragrant mix of spices.

'You would love it, Miss Brownlow,' he said. 'Your brother has told me of your longing for adventure and your discontent with this humdrum small town life.'

'He has no business discussing me behind my back,' she declared primly.

Thomas gave a sly smile. 'But it is true, is it not?'

She was unable to control the flush that rose to her cheeks. Yes, she had often dreamed of getting away from here, but her dreams had always been of sailing off into the sunset on the *Emma Jane* with Adam at the helm. A foolish dream, she knew.

'Ah, I knew it. You would love to travel abroad, wouldn't you?'

She knew what he was hinting at and tried to think of a way to change the subject.

To her relief, her brother turned to them, a glass in his hand. 'You must not monopolise our guest, Grace,' he said.

'Actually, I was trying to persuade your sister to play for us after dinner. I understand she is quite the musician.'

Grace wondered why he had to lie. After all, their conversation had been quite innocent, especially as she knew her family would not object if Thomas asked for her hand and whisked her off to India. Still, she was grateful for the interruption.

When the meal was over and they retired to the drawing room, she went across to the grand piano in the corner, busying herself with the sheets of music to hide her consternation.

As she played, she let her thoughts wander back to happier days — when her innocent childhood friendship was maturing into a deeper feeling and she looked forward to an even happier future, but then there had been the quarrel between the two families and Abel Crossley's crippling accident.

She could no longer dream of marriage to Adam and the uniting of the family businesses. She would willingly run away with him — if he asked her — but she knew he would never leave his mother and crippled father to struggle on in poverty.

She came to the end of the sonata and brought herself reluctantly back to the present. Thomas smiled approvingly and clapped his hands as she stood up to leave the piano. 'Beautifully played,

Miss Brownlow,' he said.

She smiled acknowledgement but refused to play any more. She had done her best to appear the dutiful daughter, reluctant to upset her parents. They had her best interests at heart, she knew that — and would marriage to Thomas be such a bad thing?

If she went to India with him, there would be all the excitement of discovering a new country, a different way of life. Although she knew she would never forget Adam, she would be far removed from the temptation to try and meet him in secret and possibly bring scandal upon her family. Much as she chafed against the narrow life imposed by her parents, she loved them dearly and would not want to hurt them.

Lost in thought, she hardly listened as her mother chatted to Thomas, asking him about life in India. Then her interest was piqued when she heard her mother say, 'But that's all behind you now. You've had your adventures in far off lands, and now my husband tells me you have bought a house here.'

'We are building a yacht for him too,' Charles said proudly. 'A splendid vessel with every luxury on board.'

'So, you intend to settle here, Mr Eastwood,' said Grace, her dreams of fleeing to the other side of the world fading instantly. How could she marry and remain here, so near to Adam but unable to speak to him?

'Eventually,' Thomas said in answer to Grace's question. 'But I will have to return soon to complete some business.'

James leaned across and whispered, 'A sea voyage — what a wonderful start to a honeymoon.'

Grace pushed him away, her cheeks reddening again. 'Don't talk nonsense, James.'

Elizabeth gave her son a sharp look. 'Stop teasing your sister, James,' she said, then, turning to Grace, she continued, 'I have been telling Mr Eastwood that India is not the only place where you can find exotic plants.

He is very interested in our new conservatory. Perhaps you would show him our wonderful orchids, my dear. I would come with you but I'm very tired. I think, rather than sit here listening to your father discussing business with James, I will go to bed.'

Thomas helped her to her feet and wished her goodnight before turning to Grace. 'I would very much like to see the orchids, Miss Brownlow,' he said.

Grace led the way, her heart pounding. This was the moment she had been dreading, but she would have to make her mind up one way or another. Whatever she decided her heart would break — for now she knew, however much she might dream, Adam was lost to her forever.

4

Adam looked down at his father, who was dozing in the chair by the fire. Sadly, he noticed the pallor of his cheeks, the shadows under his eyes. He had deteriorated in the past few weeks and now seldom left his chair, not even rousing himself to replenish the fire.

His mother, too, worn down by poverty and hard work had lost weight, her face drawn and lined with worry, her chestnut hair now threaded with silver.

His sadness at the change in his father was overlaid with a tinge of impatience. As he had often thought since the accident, Dad should have tried to rouse himself to find work and relieve the burden on his mother. He knew in his heart that his father couldn't help it — his illness was as much mental as physical, but it was hard to be sympathetic when he could see what it was doing to Ma.

Well, he would just have to do his part in easing the family's finances. If only he could find other work, Adam thought. Over the winter, the weather had been worse than usual, the resulting catches poor. Any day now he expected Will Symthe to tell him that he could no longer afford to employ him on the *Emma Jane*.

In contrast, the oystermen were doing well and Adam had approached one of his father's old friends, hoping to be taken on as an apprentice. He well knew it was a vain hope — the oyster trade was jealously guarded and few outsiders ever got the chance to join the Company of Free Fishers.

He didn't know what to do. The only trade he knew was boat building and he would not demean himself by asking the Brownlows for work. There were other boatyards but their owners had refused to take him on, afraid of upsetting the powerful Charles Brownlow.

After saving Grace from drowning Adam had foolishly entertained the thought that her father might soften in his attitude, but he hadn't even acknowledged his part in her rescue — not that he had expected, nor for that matter wanted, any thanks. He was just thankful he'd been there to save her.

He decided to go down to the harbour and see if any of the colliers that plied between here and Newcastle were in. Perhaps he could get taken on as a deckhand. It would mean being away from home for days or weeks on end and he was loath to leave his mother to cope with Dad on her own, but what choice did he have? It was better than joining the navy, where he might be away for years at a time.

Without telling his mother where he was going, Adam tied a knitted muffler around his neck, turned up the collar of his jacket and went out of the back gate into the alley which led between the cottages. As he emerged into the road which ran parallel to the shoreline, he shivered in the keen wind off the North Sea. He could hear the waves pounding the shore and knew there was little chance of any fishing today.

Rounding the corner by the harbour wall he noticed the masts of the moored boats tossing in the wind, but when he reached the harbour he saw that the *Emma Jane* was not among them. Will must have taken her out, despite the weather — and without asking him to go too, Adam thought. He was right then; the Smythes were feeling the pinch like many other fishermen. They could no longer afford to employ him but they were willing to risk leaving the harbour with only the two of them to man the boat. He just hoped they could manage, especially in this foul weather.

Adam hadn't expected to see anyone around and was surprised to see movement at the end of the harbour wall. He hunched his shoulders against the cold and walked quickly towards the men who were huddled over their diving equipment. The Deane brothers were famous for their pioneering work with diving helmets and waterproof suits and had travelled widely, exploring wrecks and salvaging valuable cargo. The younger brother had recently returned to set up his diving business in the little harbour town.

Adam watched the men working for a while as they untangled a mass of hose attached to the equipment which pumped air down to the divers on the seabed. One of the men looked up and said, 'Don't just stand there, lad. Lend a hand, will you?'

'What do you want me to do?' Adam asked.

The older man, whom Adam recognised as John Deane, showed him how to coil the hose, which was being whipped around by the increasing gale force wind. When it was done, he helped them to load the stuff onto a cart and made to turn away.

'Wait a minute, lad. What's your name?' the man asked.

'Adam Crossley.'

'You must be Abel's son. Well, lad, you've done a good job. Here.' He thrust a coin into Adam's hand.

Adam stammered his thanks and then dared to ask. 'What's it like — down there, under the water?'

'Interested in diving are you?'

Adam nodded.

'Why don't you come along to the Assembly Rooms tonight? I'm giving a lecture. Seven thirty.'

'I'll be there,' Adam said.

Rain had started to fall and it was getting dark when he left the divers and made his way home. It wasn't till he got indoors that he looked at the coin the man had given him, gasping with disbelief when he saw that it was a silver shilling.

'Look, Ma. I've earned some money today.' He showed her the coin and told her how he'd met Mr Deane and his partner on the harbour wall. 'He's giving a lecture tonight about diving and I'm going,' he said.

Sarah looked dismayed. 'You're not thinking of taking up diving, I hope. It's dangerous. I can't be doing with worrying about you as well as . . . ' She nodded towards the corner of the room where Abel was nodding in his chair.

Adam tried to reassure her. 'It just sounds interesting, that's all,' he told her, but in his heart he was wondering if he had finally found the means of earning a decent living and keeping his family from the workhouse.

★ ★ ★

Grace turned away from the window as the maid came to close the curtains. She had been sitting there for most of the afternoon, watching as the storm gathered intensity, and toying restlessly with the ring on her finger. The light enhanced the vivid blue of the sapphire, reminding her of Adam's eyes and the way they had always sparkled with fun and laughter.

The wind chased the purple clouds across the sky and foaming crests topped the waves. She said a mental prayer for Adam — and for all the town's fishermen who might be at sea, but surely, she told herself, they would not put out in such dreadful weather.

Since that evening a week ago when she had accepted Thomas Eastwood's marriage proposal, she had tried to put Adam out of her mind, but she couldn't help worrying about him.

She thought back to that moment in the conservatory when Thomas had asked her to be his wife. When she had hesitantly accepted, he had seized her hand and kissed it, telling her she had made him the happiest man in the world.

He had taken a small box from his pocket. 'I have been carrying this around for days, hoping for an opportunity,' he said, fumbling with the catch.

The lid sprang open and the

lamplight caught the dazzle of the multi-faceted jewel. The sapphire was huge, far more ostentatious then anything Grace had ever seen.

'It's beautiful,' she said, the words seeming inadequate, but she could not inject any enthusiasm into her voice.

Thomas didn't seem to notice. 'I thought you'd like it. It came from India, of course. Such jewels are almost commonplace out there. The Indian maharajahs festoon their women with emeralds, rubies . . . it is a sign of their wealth and importance.'

Was that why he'd chosen such a large stone, Grace thought, to impress her with his own wealth? She smiled and waited for him to say he loved her, to sweep her into his arms and kiss her. Not that she wanted him to, she told herself, but it had not been at all like the kind of proposal she had imagined and she couldn't help comparing his response with the passionate intensity of Adam's embrace.

Well, Adam had made it quite clear

that, whatever their feelings for each other, there was no future for them. At least she could hug to herself the knowledge that he loved her — but now she must make the best of things and try to look forward to the future with Thomas.

Despite her initial reservations she had to admit she enjoyed his company. Perhaps in time she would come to love him, even if not in the same way she loved Adam. And there was the voyage to India to look forward to — an exciting adventure — at least that's what she tried to tell herself.

Shutting out the storm and thoughts of Adam, Grace went to sit by the fire with her mother, who was eagerly making plans for the wedding.

'I wish we had more time to make arrangements,' she was saying now, as she pored over a magazine which contained pictures of wedding finery. 'Still, it's understandable that Thomas wants the wedding to take place so soon, since he is so eager to return to

India to complete his business before settling down here.'

Grace had hoped to postpone their marriage until he came back to England but he had insisted. 'I want to show you the wonderful sights out there before we settle down to married life,' he had said.

She had to admit, it did sound exciting, and besides, it gave her less time to think and wonder if she was doing the right thing. She sighed and tried to inject some enthusiasm into her voice as she discussed the design of her dress and how many guests they should invite.

★　★　★

The next day dawned with clear skies and a light wind. Grace prayed that the *Emma Jane* had returned safely and that the storm hadn't done too much damage.

At breakfast James and her father were talking about it too.

'We must get down to the boatyard early this morning. The tide was exceptionally high last night,' Charles said. 'Eastwood's yacht is almost complete and we could lose a lot of money if it's been damaged.'

'Don't worry, Father. I made sure everything was well battened down before I left yesterday.'

'Nevertheless, I'd like to make certain and see for myself.' He wiped his mouth with his napkin and pushed his chair back. 'Right. Come along, James. Let's not waste any more time.'

After they'd left, Grace felt a little ashamed that she hadn't voiced any concern about the boatyard. Her father was right to be worried. It was not unknown for a freak wave to reach right up to the foreshore where the half-finished boats were housed, and even to the cottages behind. The whole town beyond the harbour was vulnerable to flooding and Grace's thoughts turned again to Adam and his family in their tiny cottage.

She must find out if he was all right.

Throwing a shawl over her shoulders, she slipped out of the side door, hoping no one would see her and ask where she was going. She hurried down the hill towards the town, pausing at the harbour gate. There was still no sign of the *Emma Jane* and her heart sank. Surely the Smythes hadn't taken her out last night?

There were a lot of men around checking the damage done by the storm, but there was no sign of Billy Smythe and his father — nor of Adam. She was tempted to ask for news and was about to approach one of the fishermen when a voice hailed her.

'Miss Brownlow, what are you doing out alone? Where is your brother?' It was Thomas Eastwood.

Grace swallowed her impatient reply. Why shouldn't she be out alone? Then she reminded herself that a gentleman like Thomas would not expect a gently brought up young lady — especially his fiancée — to be wandering among the

78

rough fishermen of the town.

She forced a smile. 'James and my father have gone to inspect the boatyard,' she said. 'I wanted to see the after-effects of the storm for myself.'

'It is not as bad as we feared,' Thomas replied. 'Although I did hear that one of the fishing boats has foundered.'

Grace gave a small groan and her hand went to her throat. 'Which boat?' she asked, although she knew it her heart which one it must be.

Thomas didn't seem to notice her distress. 'I don't know. I understand the owner and his son were rescued.'

'Anyone else?' Grace asked.

'You must not concern yourself. If these men are so foolish as to take their boat out in a storm . . . '

'Foolish? You think it foolish to try to earn a living and support your family?' Her voice rose in indignation.

'Calm yourself, my dear. You misunderstood. Of course, in a small community such as this, these tragedies

79

affect everyone, but it is not your concern. Come, let me escort you home.'

He took her arm and led her away, talking all the while. He told her he'd been on his way to the boatyard to make sure his yacht was undamaged but that escorting her home was far more important. 'I cannot have my fiancée looking so distraught,' he said. 'You should be thinking happy thoughts and making plans for our wedding.' He smiled down at her and she forced a smile in return.

When they reached the gates of The Towers, she thanked him and would have taken her leave but he asked politely if he might pay his respects to her mother. She had no choice but to invite him in although she would have preferred to go straight to her room. She longed to be alone, to think about Adam — to pray for his safety.

Instead she had to sit with her mother and Thomas and make polite conversation while her emotions were in turmoil.

Uppermost in her mind was the thought that, even if Adam were drowned and lost to her for ever, she could not marry this man for whom she felt nothing at all. But she must. They were formally engaged and it was no light matter to break it off. A betrothal was almost as binding as the marriage itself.

How would Adam feel when he heard she was to be married, as he was bound to in this small town where news travelled fast and gossip was endemic?

It was a relief when Thomas finally stood up to take his leave, bowing over her hand in a gentlemanly manner. As soon as he'd gone she escaped to her room where she found Elsie sorting through her wardrobe.

'Oh, Miss,' she said. 'What shall I do with these old clothes? You won't want these heavy woollen dresses and warm furs in India.'

'I'm not going for ever, Elsie,' Grace

replied. 'Leave them in the wardrobe.'

'But I have to make room for the new things you'll be buying when you go to London next week. And you'll be bringing back stuff from India too — but of course, you'll be in your new house by then.'

Grace didn't want to think about it.

*   *   *

When Adam went down to the harbour the morning after the storm the Smythes were standing on the quayside, their face drawn with despair. The *Emma Jane* had foundered as she'd been entering the harbour and it was only by sheer good fortune that Billy and his father had not gone down with her. The tide was on the way out and, just beyond the harbour wall, the mast could be seen sticking up out of the shallow water.

Will Smythe shook his head and clapped Adam on the shoulder. 'Sorry, son. It looks like there won't be any fishing for you — or us — for a while.'

Adam didn't tell them that he had been thinking of taking on another job. 'I'm sorry too, Mr Smythe,' he said. 'What will you and Billy do?'

Will shrugged and turned away. Adam was about to follow when he saw Grace standing by the harbour gate. Although he had vowed to keep away from her, he couldn't resist the urge to approach her, but as he hurried across the quay, a man came up and spoke to her. She turned to him, smiling, and Adam's stomach churned as the man took her arm possessively and smiled down at her.

Without another glance in his direction, she walked away.

He watched them go, trying to convince himself that she couldn't have seen him or surely she would at least have wished him good morning.

He looked out to sea and brushed his hand across his eyes. It was the wind making them water, he told himself. But he couldn't dispel the cold feeling in his heart that now she would never be his. Billy Smythe had mentioned the gossip in the tavern about the rich man from India who was courting Miss Grace, and this time, it looked as if the rumours were true.

He remembered that wonderful day when they'd walked along the foreshore and he had given in to the impulse to declare his feelings. They had been happy for a few hours, each daring to hope that they would find a way to overcome their respective families' antagonism, but the reality of the situation had soon become apparent, reinforced by James Brownlow's threats.

Since then he had tried to avoid Grace, but seeing her on the arm of another man — a man she was pledged to marry — brought bitter bile to his throat. How could she so easily have forgotten those happy times together, their shared childhood and the love that had grown slowly but surely, between them?

Of course, he knew it wasn't Grace's fault. Her father had mapped out the future for his only daughter and marriage to a Crossley was not on his agenda. Adam cursed under his breath and vowed that one day he would repay the Brownlows for what they had done to him and his family.

He turned away and almost bumped into one of the men who'd been working with John Deane the previous day.

'Didn't I see you at Mr Deane's lecture last night?' he asked.

When Adam nodded, he held his hand out. 'Mick O'Brien, deep sea diver. You seem to be interested in diving.'

'It looks exciting,' Adam said.

'Well, it has its moments, but it can be plenty dangerous if you don't know what you're doing. I'm guessing you'd like to have a go, then?'

'Yes, please,' Adam said eagerly. He didn't care about danger at that moment. Did it matter what happened to him if Grace was lost to him?

'Not so fast, young man. Mr Deane won't let you go down until you've learned all about it topside. But you can give me a hand if you like.'

'I heard the divers go all over the place looking for treasure.'

Mick O'Brien gave a hearty laugh. 'I can't deny it's treasure we'd love to find. In fact, that's how I met John Deane — he was bringing up silver dollars from a ship off the Irish coast.'

Adam had heard about that — who in the town hadn't? A few years ago everyone had been talking about it.

Mr O'Brien told Adam that he'd recently been working with Mr Deane on Royal Navy wrecks in Portsmouth harbour. 'Then when he decided to come back to Kent, I came along, too.'

'Do you think he'd take me on as an assistant?' Adam asked hopefully.

'Tell you what, lad, give us a hand with this job and if you do all right, I'll put in a good word for you.' He pointed. 'That boat that went down last night — see the mast sticking up there? It's blocking the harbour entrance — a danger to the other boats. The harbour master wants it cleared.'

'That's my friend's boat,' Adam said. 'Do you really think it can be salvaged?'

'That's what we need to find out. We'd better get on with it before the tide turns and that wind gets up again.'

Adam was eager to help, pleased that he could possibly do something for his friend. He listened intently while Mr O'Brien explained the pumping mechanism which carried air down to the diver and the various signals they used to communicate while the diver was underwater.

He had paid rapt attention to last night's lecture and found that he remembered a lot of what had been said.

Mr O'Brien nodded approvingly as Adam repeated his instructions. 'You've got it, lad.'

By the time he'd finished going over it, several other men had arrived on the scene, including Mr Deane who had tied his boat up to the harbour wall. When Adam was introduced to him, he agreed that he could accompany them out to the *Emma Jane*.

He helped the men load the equipment on board and Mr Deane guided the boat through the harbour entrance to where the wreck was just visible above the water. Adam helped the diver into his suit and fastened his helmet, then Mick gave Adam the signal to start up the pump and the diver carefully let himself over the side.

Adam kept one eye on the dials of the pump while trying to see where the diver was. He followed the trail of bubbles, fascinated by the idea that the man could stay down for so long, but then snapping to attention when Mick shouted at him to pay attention. He muttered an apology and from then on concentrated on the equipment. He was determined to show that he could do the job well and hoped that by the end of the day he would have convinced Mr

Deane to take him on.

When they had finally hauled the diver up, he helped to unscrew the helmet and waited anxiously for the man's report. The man shook his head. 'No chance of bringing her up,' he said. 'She got a real battering in the storm and there's a blessed great hole in her side where she hit the harbour wall and now she's stuck fast in the mud.'

'What shall we do, Mr Deane?' Mick asked.

'Anything down there worth salvaging?' he asked the diver.

'There's the anchor and a few bits and pieces that might fetch a few bob.'

'You and Jim better get down there and bring up what you can. Then we can blast the wreck and clear the harbour entrance.' Turning to Adam, he said, 'Right, you lad, get Mick there kitted up.'

Adam helped the Irishman into his suit and for the next couple of hours was kept busy hauling the salvaged items over the side. By the time they'd cleared the wreck of the *Emma Jane* and brought up as much as they could salvage, he felt he had been working with the divers forever.

As they stowed the equipment away, he hoped that he'd earned a place in the diving team. He'd heard the men discussing their next venture — diving on a wreck across the channel in the mouth of the River Seine — and was eager to go with them.

As he climbed up the ladder to the quayside, excited to rush home and tell his parents that he'd earned a few more shillings, he heard sneering laughter and when he looked up saw James Brownlow looking down on him.

Adam became conscious that his clothes were smeared with mud and tendrils of seaweed clung to his hair where he had helped to haul the *Emma Jane's* anchor aboard.

The contrast with James in his fashionably cut coat, a snow white stock at his throat, pointed out the difference in their station in life. He had gone down while the Brownlows had steadily risen.

Nothing could have told him more clearly that he now stood no chance with Grace, especially when James gave a cruel laugh and said, 'If my little sister could see you now, Crossley ... not that she'd give you a second glance now that she is engaged to be married.' Still laughing, he walked away.

When Mr Deane asked Adam if he was willing to join them on the trip to France, sailing the following day, Adam readily agreed without a second thought. He couldn't wait to get away.

How could he stay here, where every day he ran the risk of seeing Grace and her new fiancé?

5

The next few weeks passed in a blur for Grace as first she was whisked up to London with her mother to shop for her trousseau, then endured endless fittings for her wedding dress.

She saw little of Thomas during that time and, when she finally walked on her father's arm down the aisle of the parish church, it was almost a shock to see him standing there.

Try as she would to expunge Adam from her thoughts, whenever she had pictured her wedding day it was always him she saw standing there, proud and smiling. Tears pricked her eyes as she took her place beside Thomas, thankfully hidden by her veil. She took a deep breath and blinked them away.

It was too late now. At least she had the comfort of knowing that Adam was safe — at least for the time being.

She had finally braved her brother's displeasure to ask for news of Adam, fearing the worst after the storm which had sunk the *Emma Jane*.

To her relief James told her he had not been on-board. 'But it's no use you trying to see him,' he had said with a smirk. 'He's joined those mad divers and gone off to France to try and salvage a ship's cargo.' He gave a cruel laugh. 'He didn't drown on the Smythe's boat but it's a fair bet something bad will happen while he's out there. You do realise what a dangerous occupation diving is, don't you?'

Grace had choked back a sob and James continued, 'No use crying over him, sister dear. Pull yourself together and think of your fiancé. You don't realise how lucky you are — he's a good man, rich too, and you've got a voyage to India to look forward to — I envy you, Grace.'

In other circumstances, Grace would have been excited about the forthcoming voyage. She recalled how thrilled she'd been with Thomas's descriptions of life in India. But now, as she stood beside him in the church, making her responses in a monotone, she knew she was making a terrible mistake.

When Thomas turned to her and lifted her veil to place a gentle kiss on her lips, she forced a smile. It was done, and now, she must make the best of things.

* * *

Marriage wasn't a bit how Grace had imagined. At least, that part of it wasn't. She wasn't ignorant of the facts of life and thought she knew what to expect, but Thomas had been surprisingly thoughtful, leaving her alone in their room at the inn, where they were spending the first night of their married life.

'I'm sure you must be tired after such a long day,' he had said, kissing her gently on the forehead and leaving the room.

She had been grateful for his sensitivity but, she had to admit, a little disappointed too, anxious to be done with what she thought of as an ordeal.

The ship sailed the next day from Southampton and, over the next few days, despite the weather being fine and the passage smooth, several passengers became ill. Grace remained healthy however, and spent her time up on deck, taking in the sights and sounds of life on board a large vessel. Although she'd lived all her life by the sea and was familiar with small boats, this was her first real sea voyage and she was revelling in the experience. She had become used to washing in salt water, as well as the smells and sounds of the livestock on board.

If it hadn't been for her continued disquiet over her relationship — or lack of it — with her new husband, she would have been enjoying herself. Hidden deep within her and scarcely acknowledged was the thought of how different it would be if only Adam were with her.

Thomas mostly left her to her own devices except when politeness dictated that he should join her and the other passengers for meals or for the endless games of whist with which they passed the time. Alone in their cabin he was polite and friendly but he didn't treat her as she had expected a man would treat a new wife.

Although in some ways relieved, Grace began to wonder if there was something wrong with her. Why had he married her? It could not be for her wealth. After all, he was a rich man in his own right. As she leaned against the rail watching the sun glinting on the waves, breathing deeply of the fresh sea air and enjoying the feel of the breeze in her hair, she fingered the ruby necklace Thomas had given her on their wedding day, one of the many items of jewellery he had lavished on her — she had left most of it behind, worried about such valuable possessions being stolen or lost.

As they journeyed south the heat had increased and their cabin was like an oven. She wished she could stay up here on deck for ever but it was time to go below and dress for dinner. For the next two hours she smiled and pretended that she was a happy newly-wed while Thomas accepted compliments on his beautiful new bride and kissed her hand as if he were the happiest man in the world. If only they knew, she thought, looking round at the smiling faces.

Back in their cabin she decided to be brave and broach the subject, but he shook his head impatiently and said, 'What is it, Grace? I'm tired.'

She lost her nerve and made a remark about how enjoyable the meal had been. 'Not what I expected on board ship.'

'Not that enjoyable. You scarcely ate a thing,' he said.

She didn't reply, just carried on

getting ready for bed, brushing her hair and leaving it loose so that it gleamed in the lamplight. She put on the flimsy robe her mother had picked out for her honeymoon and turned to Thomas with a forced smile.

He seemed to look right through her and when she climbed into their bunk, he went towards the door. 'It's too hot to sleep. I'm going up for a breath of air,' he said.

'But I thought you were tired . . . ' Her words fell on empty air and she turned towards the wall, stifling her sobs in her pillow.

Although she couldn't bear the thought of Thomas touching her in that way, she had been prepared to accept it. After all, if she wanted children she would have to put up with that distasteful act, as her mother had called it. And she did want a child — it was the only thing that would make this farce of a marriage bearable — but it would never happen if her husband continued to treat her so coldly.

After a few minutes she pulled herself together and sat up. 'No use crying,' she muttered to herself, turning her pillow over, and trying to find a cool spot. Thomas was right; it was too hot to sleep. Perhaps things would be different when they returned to England and were settled in their new home.

Sleep still did not come and she got up, wrapping a shawl round her shoulders. Despite the heat, she couldn't be seen wandering around the ship in her flimsy robe, but she had to get some air. She crept along the companionway and up the steps to the lower deck. Several of the passengers had taken their bedding up here to try and gain a little relief from the heat. To her relief they all seemed sound asleep.

None of the crew was around and there was no sign of Thomas either. There was little wind and the ship seemed to be scarcely moving. Grace could hear the sailors calling to each other as they manipulated the sails to make the most of the slight breeze. It was still hot but a little cooler than the cabin and she leaned against the rail, hidden from view by one of the ship's lifeboats.

The stars in their unfamiliar constellations seemed so much brighter here far out on the ocean and Grace was entranced by the beauty of the scene. She had tried to share these thoughts with Thomas in the early days of the voyage but he seemed to have no interest in anything she had to say. How he had changed since their first meeting when he had enchanted her with tales of India and the mysterious east. Grace could not stifle the involuntary thought of how different this voyage would be if Adam were here.

She sighed and was about to go back to her cabin when she heard a man's voice. She shrank back into the shadows, hoping that whoever it was would go away.

'You could have knocked me down with a feather when I saw your name on the passenger list,' the man said. He gave a coarse laugh. 'And with a lovely new bride too.'

Grace stiffened and waited tensely for the reply. 'Yes, I'm a very lucky man,' Thomas said.

'I'll say, but you're running a bit of a risk going back, aren't you?' the other man said.

'I don't know what you're implying,' Thomas said stiffly.

'Come on, old boy. You know perfectly well what I'm getting at. You did the right thing leaving when you did. I never thought you'd be stupid enough to return.'

'Unfinished business. Besides, I won't be staying in Calcutta for long. I have to go up country, sort a few things out and then it's back to the old country for me — for good this time.'

'Then why bring your wife, Eastwood? Couldn't you have left her behind?'

'I have my reasons,' Thomas said.

Grace shoved her fist in her mouth, biting her knuckles as she waited for him to elaborate, but the men moved off, their voices and footsteps fading away. When she was sure they'd gone, she crept from her hiding place and scurried back to the cabin, hoping Thomas wouldn't reach it before her.

He wasn't there and she got into bed, staring at the door and willing him to enter. Should she tell him what she'd overheard, ask him what it meant? Recalling her husband's angry tone she didn't think it was a good idea.

For the rest of the night she lay awake, wondering if he was mixed up in something shady as the man had implied. If so, surely he'd have been better sorting things out on his own without the encumbrance of a wife. It wasn't as if he had fallen madly in love with her and couldn't bear to leave her behind — given their relationship so far, why had he even been so keen to get married in the first place?

As the first light brightened the porthole she fell into an uneasy doze, resolving that, short of confronting

Thomas directly, she would do her best to find out what was going on.

★ ★ ★

Adam had taken to his new job with enthusiasm. He hadn't yet been allowed to don the diving suit and helmet and go underwater but he was finding the whole business fascinating. He was a willing pupil and Mick O'Brien had taken him under his wing, promising that as soon as he had learned enough he could do a practice dive in shallow water.

'It's too dangerous here,' Mick said when Adam once more badgered him about it. 'There's strong currents that could sweep you away, not to mention the possibility of getting tangled in the wreckage.'

When Adam protested, he went on, 'You'll get your chance, lad. I can see you're keen — and don't worry, you'll get your share of the booty.'

It wasn't just the money he could

earn that was driving Adam; he'd developed a genuine interest in deep sea diving. He had enjoyed working in the boatyard with his father as a small boy and if things had been different would have gladly followed him into the business when he was old enough to be apprenticed, but he was beginning to realise that this was a far more interesting occupation.

Not only that, he had soon realised that, with luck, he could earn enough to help his family out of poverty and perhaps even be in a position to overcome the Brownlows' opposition and marry Grace. He refused to believe that, whatever James might have told him, she would give in to her family's pressure and actually marry Eastwood.

Adam resolved that when he returned to England he would speak to her father. He would have to curb his hatred and accept that the loss of his family's business had not entirely been Charles Brownlow's fault. All he had done was take over their debts — and their business — and stop the family ending up in the workhouse, and he had no real proof that James had been responsible for his father's accident. Surely his love for Grace could help him to overcome his bitterness.

★　★　★

The dive went well and they managed to bring up most of the French ship's cargo as well as some spars, blocks and pulleys which could be sold to a ship builder. Adam's share of the money was far more than he'd anticipated and it was with a light heart that he leapt off the boat onto the quayside and hurried through the narrow streets to his home.

At this rate, he thought, his mother would be able to give up taking in other people's washing, and they would eventually be able to afford the very best medical care for his father.

Mr Deane confirmed he was now a permanent member of the team and promised that before the next voyage he would be instructed in the use of the diving suit. If he proved to have an aptitude for it he would make his first real dive on the next wreck they went to. As well as excitement at the chance of going below the waves and exploring sunken wrecks, Adam knew that those who did the actual diving received a bigger share of the proceeds. He could soon be a rich man and then no one could say he wasn't good enough to marry a Brownlow.

He ran down the alley at the side of the house and burst through the back door. 'I'm home, Ma, Dad!' he shouted, throwing his bag down in a corner of the scullery and going through to the kitchen.

His father had been dozing in his usual chair in front of the range and he stirred and smiled. 'Welcome home, son.' His voice was faint and Adam felt the exuberance drain out of him. Abel seemed to have shrunk in the weeks he'd been away. Was he getting weaker?

He turned a worried face to his

mother. She put the iron she'd been using back on the range and folded the pillowcase she was working on. Her welcoming smile seemed forced, but she reached over and touched his cheek. 'Good to have you home, son,' she said.

'It's good to be home, Ma.' He dived into his coat pocket and pulled out a small leather bag, tipping the contents out on to the scrubbed deal table.

Sarah's eyes widened as the coins tumbled out and she laughed. 'Look at that, Dad — our lad's struck it rich!'

'Not exactly rich, Ma, but it's better than the fishing.'

'Sit down, Adam. I'll get you something to eat.' She pushed him into the chair on the other side of the range and he sat down with a sigh of content. Thrilling as it had been to travel across the sea to France, as well as working with Mick and Mr Deane, it was good to be home with his family.

He looked across at his father who had closed his eyes again and once more a feeling of dread stole over him. Had the change in the family's fortunes come too late to help him?

His mother had gone through to the scullery and returned with a kettle full of water which she placed on the range. She took a small piece of cold meat and a loaf from the larder and cut a couple of slices. 'Get that down you, son,' she said. 'I'll soon have a hot drink made for you.'

He pulled his chair up to the table. 'Have you both eaten already?' he asked, worried that he was taking the food from their mouths.

Sarah glanced at Abel and nodded. 'Your dad doesn't need much feeding these days,' she said quietly.

Adam was about to speak but she put her hand on his arm. 'Don't fret, son. He's been in such pain lately. I think he's ready to let go now.'

'No, Ma. We can get him a good doctor now.' Adam almost choked on a sob.

'It's too late for doctors. Maybe they

could have done something when he was first hurt . . . ' Her voice trailed off and she sank down at the table opposite him, her head in her hands.

The joy in his homecoming faded away and all Adam's old hatred of the Brownlows flooded back, despite his vow to put the past behind him — and where did that leave him as regards Grace? Could their love for each other overcome the bitterness between the two families?

The next day he was glad he had not rushed up the hill to The Towers to try and see Grace the minute he'd stepped off the boat. He had got up early and helped his mother to bath Abel and make him comfortable, noting with a sinking heart how frail his father had become during his short absence.

His mother smiled sadly. 'We're lucky to have had him for so long, but there's nothing we can do for him now, son, except keep him warm and comfortable.'

Adam couldn't bear to stay in the

house and he fled down to the harbour. The fishing fleet and the oyster dredgers were visible out on the open sea, the harbour almost empty of craft. Will Smythe and Billy were standing on the quayside looking out to sea too.

'No fishing today?' Adam said.

'Not without a boat. None of them need extra crew. The insurance money's taking it's time and meanwhile me and the missus and kids have to eat,' said Will.

'Thank goodness you were insured though. Will you get another boat?'

'Already on the stocks at Brownlows. They've started work and agreed to defer payment until the money comes through.'

Adam gritted his teeth at the mention of the Brownlows — they weren't being kind in offering to defer payment. They knew very well that if the money wasn't forthcoming, they could sell the boat to another customer. He just hoped his friends would get their insurance money in time, but he forced himself to smile and express his pleasure that things would eventually work out for them.

'I'll have a word with Mr Deane,' he said, turning to Billy. 'He's got several diving boats now so maybe he could do with an extra pair of hands.'

'Have you been down in one of them diving helmets yet?' Billy asked eagerly.

Adam shook his head. 'Next trip I will, though.'

'Don't fancy it myself, but I'm good with a boat as you know.'

'I'll tell him then.'

He was about to walk away when Billy said, 'You missed all the excitement while you were away . . . big wedding — that Miss Brownlow you pulled out of the harbour that day, she married that rich bloke and went off to India with him.'

Suddenly Adam's chest felt tight and he found it hard to breath. Grace married? Gone to India? Although James had taunted him with the news that she was engaged, he hadn't really believed she would actually go through with the marriage.

These past few weeks he'd really felt that things were changing for him. He had been elated at the thought of coming home with money in his pocket — both for his parents and for his future prospects as a suitor for his childhood sweetheart.

Now, in just one day he had been brought down to earth with a vengeance — first the news of his father's deteriorating health and now this . . .

What else could go wrong, he wondered.

6

They had been at sea for more than a month now and Grace was longing for the voyage to come to an end. Perhaps things between her and Thomas would improve once they were settled in their own home.

'Will it be this hot when we get there?' she asked. The heat on board ship, although mitigated by the breeze, had now become unbearable. Grace had suggested to Thomas that they join the passengers who had elected to sleep in the open but he had insisted that she stay in their cabin.

She had occasionally slipped up on deck while Thomas was still in the saloon drinking or playing cards and she never tired of looking up at the unfamiliar constellations in the blue-black sky. But her sense of adventure was beginning to pall and she longed for home. Even the cold gales off the North Sea would be preferable to this debilitating weather.

'It will be the cool season by the time we reach Calcutta and if my business goes well we should be on our way home in a couple of months — well before the heat builds up again.'

Before their marriage Thomas had been rather vague about how he'd made his fortune and Grace had not been sufficiently interested to ask. Now she recalled that overheard conversation and her curiosity was aroused.

'What business is it, Thomas?' she asked.

He laughed. 'Nothing you would understand, my dear,' he said. 'It is something best left to the men, as I'm sure your mother taught you.'

She was furious at his patronising tone and said, 'But I'm really interested, Thomas.'

As she'd known he would, he simply changed the subject, telling her that he had rented a type of house called a bungalow on the outskirts of Calcutta, the home of a couple who had gone back to England on leave.

'It is already furnished and the servants have been looking after things. My friend assures me that they are all very reliable and will try to make life easy for you when we arrive there.'

'Do they speak English?' she asked.

'Ranjit, the head boy does — he's a sort of butler and oversees the household. The cook and the other servants only know a few words.'

Grace wondered how she would manage to communicate when Thomas was out of the house.

He tried to reassure her, saying she would soon get the hang of things, but she had become friendly with an officer's wife who was returning after accompanying her two children to school in England. Mrs Johnson had tried to prepare her for life as an Englishwoman in India and the picture she painted was not as rosy as Thomas's.

Grace learned that there were strict rules governing the wives of the men who had made their careers in that far off country.

'You will find it very strange at first, my dear,' Mrs Johnson said as they sat in their deckchairs under an awning, trying to make the most of the cool morning air before the sun rose higher in the brassy sky.

She went on to explain the proper way to address the Indian servants and taught Grace a few words of the language which would help her in making her commands understood.

'My husband tells me the head boy speaks English and is very reliable.'

'Nevertheless, you have to be very firm with them, Mrs Eastwood. They seem to sense if you are nervous and unsure of yourself and they will take advantage, believe me.'

Grace didn't like the sound of that. Although they had servants at home she had known most of them since childhood and felt comfortable with them. She never gave orders anyway — just asked them politely to do what she wanted. She felt a sudden wave of longing for her old nurse, who had become more of a companion and confidante in recent years. If only she'd been able to bring her on the voyage too.

Since the night she'd overheard Thomas's conversation with one of the other passengers she had studied them all carefully but had been unable to recognise the man he'd been talking to. The men on board were either soldiers returning after leave or civil servants and government officials. None of them seemed to pay Thomas much attention and he only acknowledged them as passing shipboard acquaintances — at least when she was in his company. Why was he being so secretive? And why, if he didn't want her to know what he was up to, had he brought her with him at all?

* * *

The ship docked at Cape Town for a couple of days and Grace went ashore with Mrs Johnson. She was charmed by the pretty houses set in their neat gardens and the hospitality of the Dutch settlers, such that when it was time to go back on board ship, she almost wished she could stay behind.

Mrs Johnson's stories of life for English women in Calcutta now held no allure for her. The excitement she had originally felt at the start of the voyage had dulled to a feeling almost amounting to dread. She could only be thankful that, unlike Mrs Johnson, she was not to spend years there.

After leaving Cape Town, the weather became hotter still and Grace wondered how cool the 'cool season' could possibly be if this was what life in the tropics was like. She spent the days in her cabin, sinking into lethargy, lacking the energy to join the other ladies in the saloon. Besides, she was bored with their constant gossiping and bickering.

In the evenings when it was a little

cooler, she went up on deck to watch the whales and porpoises frolicking alongside the ship, a sight that cheered her a little. As darkness fell, the Southern Cross glowed in the sky and a silvery trail of phosphorous sparkled in the ship's wake. Thomas seldom joined her and, as she stood at the rail, her thoughts inevitably turned to Adam and how she would have revelled in these wonderful sights if only he were at her side.

★ ★ ★

At last, after nine weeks at sea, they sighted land and Grace couldn't wait to go ashore, but the voyage was not yet over as the ship made its laborious way up the River Hooghly, navigating between miles of treacherous sand-banks.

Mrs Johnson came to join her as she leaned on the ship's rail taking in the scenery, enchanted by the sight of the lush date and coconut palms lining the river bank and between them occasional glimpses of cool green rice fields. Perhaps life in this beautiful new country wouldn't be so bad after all, she thought, only to be disillusioned when her new friend said, 'I do hope we get there in one piece. Ships are always running aground on these sandbanks.'

She decided to stay up on deck until they docked, petrified at the thought of being trapped below in her cabin if the ship should founder. However, the rest of the voyage passed without incident and when they docked at Calcutta all was noise and bustle, the sailors running up and down the rigging furling the sails, as the officers shouted orders. Small boats pulled alongside, the natives shouting their wares and adding to the cacophony, and Grace felt her old optimism return with the exciting scenes.

The passengers, after frantically gathering their belongings together, rushed up on deck, hanging over the ship's rail and waving to friends and family who had come to greet them. On the quayside, scantily dressed labourers swung bales of cotton on to the waiting ships, while men in European dress hustled them to work faster. Amidst all the noise and colour, Grace became aware of the strange smells which hung in the air.

She wrinkled her nose and Mrs Johnson, standing beside her, said, 'Spices, my dear, and other things which I won't mention. You do get used to it — after a while you won't even notice it.'

Grace wasn't so sure and she held a handkerchief to her nose. 'What *is* that?' she asked.

'Burning cow dung — they use it for fuel,' Thomas said, laughing as she shuddered. 'Don't be silly Grace. It's no worse than the smell of fish back home,' he said.

It was true that visitors to her home town often complained of the fishy smell, especially near the harbour, but she had grown up with it. Perhaps Mrs

Johnson was right and she would get used to it. Besides, she'd done a lot of thinking during those lonely hours on board ship and she had decided that the only way she could cope with things was to embrace the differences and treat this period of her life as an adventure. She would learn all she could about this strange country and try to enjoy the experience — even the heat and the smells.

Although Grace was looking forward to settling into her new home, Mrs Johnson had warned her that it would not be what she was used to.

'They are not like European houses,' she explained. 'The kitchen is usually in a separate building behind the house, and there's a thatched veranda all round — it helps to keep the place cool.' She smiled reassuringly. 'You will be quite comfortable, but you must watch out for snakes and insects.'

Grace shuddered and her friend laughed. 'Don't worry, my dear, you will soon get used to them. It's true they do lurk in the roof and sometimes drop down from above but there are awnings stretched across the ceiling to catch them and the servants are very vigilant.'

It all sounded very primitive to Grace so she was somewhat relieved when Thomas told her they would be spending a night at the Imperial Hotel in Calcutta.

As they left the crowded harbour and approached along Chowringhee, the principle street of the city, she gazed in awe at the buildings, most of them built of red brick in the classical style. She had not expected to see so many shops, hotels and civic buildings.

★   ★   ★

Grace slept well and woke feeling refreshed after her first night for weeks in a proper bed. There was no sign of Thomas so, very nervously, she went down to the dining room alone, hoping to find him already there.

As she paused in the doorway, looking round for him, a servant or porter came towards her holding an envelope.

'Good morning Mrs Eastwood. I hope you slept well. Your husband asked me to give you this. He regrets he had to leave early and did not wish to disturb you.' He led her to a table and waited until she was seated before moving discreetly away.

She opened the note and quickly scanned the contents. There were no endearments, the tone was formal, almost cold.

I regret that I have to go up country on business. Someone will take you to the bungalow. Our luggage has already been sent on there and the servants will see to it. I hope to be back in a few days.

He had signed it Thomas Eastwood — not your loving husband or even just Thomas; nothing to indicate that they were more than mere acquaintances. Which is what they were, she supposed, given the bad start to their married life.

She choked back a sob, wondering how she could ever have agreed to marry him, still less travel halfway across the world with this man who was almost a stranger. The engaging young man who had entertained her with such colourful tales of his travels and adventures now seemed like a different person.

She had imagined that they would explore the country together. Surely, even if she could never bring herself to feel the same way about him as she did about Adam, she could have enjoyed his company as a friend and companion, and if he would let her, she would have done her best to be a good wife.

How could she have been so deceived? Worse, how could she have been so foolish as to deceive herself?

The fact that he could go off and leave her alone in a strange country with no idea how to get to their new home and no indication of when he would return, spoke volumes of his disregard for her feelings. She dried the tears which were beginning to well up and resolved to go back to her room and write to her parents straightaway. They would not let her be treated like this, she was sure.

She would ask them to send James to fetch her home. After all, despite the fact that she and Thomas had exchanged vows in church, it was not a true marriage. She would just have to overcome her embarrassment at the situation and explain why.

She waved the hovering waiter away and stood up to leave the table. It was too hot to eat. Already the air was humid despite the ceiling fans which Mrs Johnson had told her were called punkahs. They created a breeze it was true but it was merely a stirring of the hot air and did little to make her more comfortable, dressed as she still was in her heavy European clothes. As she left the dining room, she met Mrs Johnson on her way in.

'Have you breakfasted already?' the

older woman asked. 'And what about your husband?'

'He's been called away on business,' Grace replied, unable to suppress the catch in her throat.

'You mean he's left you here alone — on your first day in the city? Oh, you poor thing!' Mrs Johnson took her arm. 'Now, you must join me at my table. I am expecting my friends to join me in a day or two to escort me up country. Meanwhile I'm at a loose end so I shall take great pleasure in showing you the ropes.' She led Grace back to the table she had just vacated and beckoned imperiously to a waiter.

Within minutes a selection of dishes had been brought and, when Mrs Johnson complained about the heat, a punkah wallah was summoned to stand behind them and discreetly manipulate a smaller fan to supplement the ceiling fans.

On board ship, Grace had sometimes found the older woman a bit overbearing but today she was grateful for a friendly face. She confided that Thomas expected her to leave the hotel for the bungalow and said that she would much rather stay in the hotel until he returned.

'Nonsense, my dear. You can't stay here alone. I'll come with you and see you settled in.' She looked round at the other hotel guests, then turned back to Grace. 'I was hoping to bump into some people I know — it would help if you had some introductions. Still, I daresay, once people know there is a newcomer they will call and leave their cards.'

She finished eating and smiled at Grace. 'I hope your husband told you to pack riding clothes. Everyone rides on the maidan — early in the morning before it gets too hot.'

Grace did not want to confess that she did not ride so she asked, 'What is the maidan?'

'It's a big open space, like a park. You could almost be back home. Your husband will take you when he returns from his business.' She replaced her cup in the saucer and pushed her chair back. 'I'll go and see what arrangements Mr Eastwood has made for you. Run up to your room and pack, my dear. I'll wait for you here.'

★　★　★

The bulk of their luggage had already been delivered straight to the house and it did not take Grace long to pack her few belongings. When she returned to the lounge, Mrs Johnson was talking to a European couple whom Grace did not remember seeing on board ship. Perhaps these were the friends who had come to meet Mrs Johnson. It seemed she might have to make her own way to her new home, she thought, hesitating in the doorway until Mrs Johnson turned and caught sight of her.

'Come and be introduced, my dear,' she called. 'Mr Wilmot is stationed here in Calcutta. You'll probably see quite a bit of them once you're settled.'

Grace shook hands with the couple, who both looked at her with frank curiosity.

'Eastwood? Are you by any chance related to Colonel Eastwood?' asked Mr Wilmot.

'He was my husband's father. I never had the chance to meet him before he died,' Grace replied. In fact, Thomas had told her very little of his background, save that he had been born in India and that his parents were both dead.

'Your husband? You are married to Thomas Eastwood?' Mrs Wilmot said, her eyebrows raised in surprise.

'Mrs Eastwood is on her honeymoon. She and Thomas married in England,' Mrs Johnson said.

'But I thought . . . ?'

'I believe Thomas intended to stay in England but it seems a matter of business has brought him back, and Mrs Eastwood had a longing to see the country,' Mrs Johnson interrupted.

'We won't be here long but perhaps

we'll meet again,' Grace said, smiling at her new acquaintances.

'Perhaps.' Mrs Wilmot did not return the smile. She took her husband's arm. 'We really must be going, dear,' she said, turning to Mrs Johnson. 'Give our regards to your husband.'

They hurried away, leaving Mrs Johnson staring after them with a puzzled expression. 'I wonder why they were in such a hurry. It's not like Letty to forgo the chance of a conversation with a newcomer. She is always avid for news from England.'

'Perhaps they had another engagement,' Grace said. But she had noticed the change of expression on Mrs Wilmot's face when she had mentioned Thomas.

'Yes, that must be it,' Mrs Johnson agreed hastily, taking her arm. 'Well, come along, the cart is here.'

Outside the hotel, a bullock cart was waiting for them and Grace climbed up a little nervously. 'Are there no carriages?' she asked.

'Some have their own private carriages, but these carts are better suited to the rough roads,' Mrs Johnson said. She pointed to an elephant moving ponderously towards them, its passenger seated in a boxlike contraption on its back. 'You could always hire one of those,' she said, smiling mischievously.

Grace shuddered as the passenger swayed dangerously from side to side. She had to admit she felt safer in the sturdy cart.

As the Indian driver forced his way along the street crowded with cows, dogs and beggars, she became almost overwhelmed by the noise which made conversation impossible. Above the creaking of the cart there was an incessant stream of voices in strange languages and the raucous cries of vividly coloured parrots. Adding to the colourful scene were the women in their saris of turquoise, orange and bright pink, some adorned with jewellery and with flowers in their hair.

They did not seem to feel the heat

and Grace wished she was dressed like them instead of in her European dress with its many heavy layers. She resolved that the first thing she would do when she reached the bungalow would be to remove her corsets. She didn't care what anyone might think; she would faint if she had to put up with them any longer.

Leaving the wide main thoroughfare, they entered a narrow street of Indian houses and tenements and she began to be apprehensive. What would this 'bungalow' be like?

It was a great relief when they reached the European residential quarter and she saw the neat rows of single story houses with their shady gardens. It was nothing like home but she was relieved to be away from the noisy, smelly city centre.

The head boy greeted them at the foot of the steps leading up to the wide veranda, calling a couple of other servants to take the luggage.

'I am Ranjit,' he said, bowing over

clasped hands. 'I have refreshments ready for you.'

Grace thanked him and entered the bungalow, looking around with interest at her new home. It was unlike any building she'd ever encountered before. Instead of glass, the window openings had blinds to keep out the sun and shutters to close at night. 'Much cooler than proper windows,' Mrs Johnson told her.

She hurried from room to room, exclaiming at the furnishings and the muslin drapes around the bed and asking Mrs Johnson why the bed legs were standing in tins of water.

'That's to stop insects crawling up,' she said, smiling at Grace's look of horror.

'Don't worry. The servants are instructed to check everywhere before you retire for the night. This is just a precaution. The natives don't seem to worry but we Europeans are obviously not used to it.'

Grace didn't want to get used to it.

Fascinated as she was by the country and its customs, determined to embrace her new experiences, she did not think she would ever find creepy crawlies and snakes interesting.

Although Thomas had told her that the bungalow was furnished, she was dismayed by the sparseness of the interior. The rooms only contained the most basic necessities. Perhaps the owners had put their best furniture in storage while they were away, she thought.

'Men don't know about these things,' her friend said. 'Tomorrow I'll take you shopping. If you are going to be here for any length of time you will be entertaining and you will need a dinner set, dishes and tablecloths and suchlike.'

Grace couldn't imagine who she would be inviting to dinner since she didn't know anybody apart from Mrs Johnson who would shortly be departing to join her husband. Besides, her stay was only going to be temporary.

After exploring the house, she and her friend went outside to look at the grounds. In front of the bungalow was an area of beaten earth but beyond that was the garden. Grace's spirits rose at the sight of the colourful flowers and shrubs. Mrs Johnson couldn't tell her their names but she recognised some as similar to the blooms that were growing in the conservatory of The Towers.

They brought a pang of homesickness, which she quickly tried to suppress when Mrs Johnson told her it was time for lunch, which her friend told her was known as 'tiffin'. They returned to the house and sat in the shade on the veranda and Grace soon realised why she needed the fly whisk which Thomas had bought for her on the way to the hotel.

She sat back in her chair with a sigh, hoping that he would soon get back from his trip up country, wherever that might be. She didn't think she'd ever get used to the heat and the strange ways of this place and the sooner he finished his business and they could go home, the better. She decided she'd already seen enough of India.

A servant came in on noiseless feet and set the huge brass tray on the table between them, retreating as quietly as he'd come. As she poured tea and handed the delicate bone china cup and saucer to her friend, she pondered over the encounter with the Wilmots, wondering why they had ended the conversation so abruptly. They had seemed disposed to be friendly until she had mentioned her husband.

Taking a deep breath, she asked Mrs Johnson, 'Have you known the Wilmots long?'

'Yes, they've been out here almost as long as I have. Mr Wilmot travels all over the country but Letty usually stays at their house up in the hills. She rarely comes to the city.'

'How do they know my husband?' she asked.

'I believe they had a business connection.'

Grace did not ask what that might be. She didn't want to confess how little she knew of her husband's background or why it had been necessary for him to return to India.

'Mrs Wilmot didn't seem very friendly,' she said.

'No doubt she has her reasons.' Mrs Johnson put her hand over her mouth. 'I'm so sorry, I did not mean to speak so sharply.' She leaned forward and patted Grace's hand. 'Take no notice of her, my dear. There is a great deal of snobbery here. Everyone has their place and it is difficult to fit in sometimes.'

Grace wasn't satisfied. 'I get the feeling it is my husband they do not like.'

'I'm sure you're wrong.'

'I don't think so. Besides, if there is something I should know . . . ' Grace was thinking back to that overheard conversation on board ship. She decided to tell Mrs Johnson about it and ask her advice. If she was going to be here for any length of time it was surely better for her to be aware of any possible unpleasantness.

Mrs Johnson listened in silence as Grace poured out her doubts and suspicions of her husband. When she'd finished, the older woman sighed.

'There was some talk on board ship but I hoped you had not heard anything. After all, you plan to go home quite soon so there is no need . . . ' She paused.

'I would rather know. Thomas has said very little about his business here and why he had to return.'

'It would have been better if you had stayed in England. I can't think why he insisted you accompany him.'

'It is supposed to be our honeymoon,' Grace said with a little catch in her voice. She put her cup down. 'Please if you know anything at all . . . '

'I don't like to pass on gossip — it is a besetting sin of the women out here. They have so little to occupy them that chattering about the goings-on of their neighbours seems to be their chief pastime. When someone new arrives they make it their business to find out all about them and their background.' She sighed. 'I suppose I must tell you. You probably didn't hear as you kept to your cabin most of the time. Someone who knew your husband out here recognised him and told another passenger. The word soon spread.'

'What word? What has my husband done?'

'I'm not sure exactly but he left India under a cloud — something to do with mismanagement of funds.'

'Stealing you mean?' Grace was horrified.

Mrs Johnson hastened to reassure her. 'It may not be as bad as that. I told you I wasn't sure. All I am sure of is that it was a mistake for him to come back. The British community out here is really quite small and everyone knows everyone else. It will be hard for you to fit in once word gets around.'

'I don't want to fit in,' Grace declared. 'Besides, we're going back to

England quite soon.' She choked back a sob. 'I don't understand why he brought me with him. Why didn't he postpone our wedding?'

'I suspect it was a defiant gesture on his part — to show that he was a respectable married man, that he had been accepted into English society. After all, as far as I can make out, nothing was proved against him — he left the country before proceedings could be taken.'

Grace managed a smile. 'I'm surprised you want to be friends with me,' she said.

'You aren't to blame for what your husband might have done and everyone needs a friend when they arrive in this country. I can't tell you how homesick and bewildered I was when I arrived all those years ago.'

The two women sat and chatted for a while and Grace began to feel a bit better. She resolved that when Thomas returned she would tackle him about what she'd discovered and force him to tell her the truth. She didn't want to believe he had done anything dishonest and she wondered if she'd be able to forgive him if she found out that he had. She was sure her family would be just as shocked and dismayed as she was at being so easily taken in by him.

She felt quite bereft when Mrs Johnson announced she must return to the hotel to find out if there was any message from her friends. 'If you need anything, just send a boy with a note,' she said, referring to the servants.

Grace said goodbye, feeling fortunate that they'd met — she might need friends in the days to come. But as she wandered through the empty rooms of the bungalow, she reminded herself that Mrs Johnson would soon be departing for her own home, many miles away. And then she'd be all alone.

7

A few days later, still no one had come to call and there had been no word from Thomas either. For the first couple of days Grace had been taken up with the newness of everything and had spent the time trying to converse with the servants and to learn a little about how the household was run.

She was mindful of Mrs Johnson's warning to be firm but how could she be sure she was handling things correctly when she didn't know the language?

The head boy, Ranjit, seemed anxious to please and Grace found herself relying on him to communicate her orders to the cook and the other servants.

If she tried to do anything for herself, such as clear the dishes away after a meal, he gently dissuaded her, explaining that the boys would feel insulted.

Grace hated being idle and, becoming bored, she wandered out into the garden, admiring the lush blooms. There were vines with huge trumpet-like flowers in bright yellow and red, entwined with purple passion flowers which she recognised as similar to those that grew in the conservatory at home. She noticed that the leaves on one of the plants were discoloured and shrivelled and she bent to examine them more closely.

Startled, she straightened when a voice shouted, 'No, memsahib, no.'

Thinking that some poisonous insect was lurking among the leaves, she jumped back. 'What is it?' she cried.

The gardener came towards her, waving his hands and gabbling. From the few garbled English words among the strange sounds she realised he was trying to tell her that it was his job to look after the garden. If the memsahib wanted flowers for the house, he would cut them for her and bring them indoors.

She managed to smile, ashamed of her fearful reaction. 'Thank you. I would like some flowers,' she said, hoping that he had understood.

She retreated to the veranda and called for Ranjit. 'I fear that I have insulted the mali,' she said, pleased that she had remembered the word for gardener. 'I did not intend to.' She sighed. 'I will never learn the correct ways.' She knew she should not have revealed her true feelings in front of the servant, but there was no one else to talk to.

He seemed sympathetic and begged her to consult him if she wasn't sure of anything. 'Our ways are strange to you, but you will soon learn, memsahib.' His words could have seemed over familiar but his tone was respectful and Grace found herself warming to him.

Arranging the flowers, a task she had always found boring when at home in England, at least filled in some of the lonely hours. She asked Anish, the mali, to bring her fresh ones each day, pleased when she was able to make herself understood. Ordering the meals and inspecting the stores, making sure that the cook boiled all the water that was used for cooking, also helped to pass the time.

Nevertheless she longed for the company of her own kind and, when there was still no word from Thomas, she sent one of the boys to the hotel with a note for Mrs Johnson inviting her to call. She hoped her friend had not already left the city and was relieved when the boy returned with a note saying that she would call later that day.

★　★　★

When Mrs Johnson stepped down from the cart, Grace greeted her warmly, feeling a rush of affection for the kindly older woman — and after all, hers was the first European face she'd seen for days.

'I'm so pleased you could come,' she

said. 'I was afraid you might have left already.'

'As if I would leave without coming to say goodbye,' Mrs Johnson said, as Grace led her into the dim drawing room, its shades drawn against the glaring sun. She looked round approvingly, nodding towards the flower arrangements dotted around on small tables. 'You are already turning this into a home,' she said.

They sat down and Grace summoned a boy and ordered tea. 'Is there any news of your friends?' she asked Mrs Johnson.

'They've been delayed so I shall be here for a little while longer,' the older woman replied.

'I'm sorry to hear that — you must be longing to get home.' The word home stuck in Grace's throat. How could anyone think of this alien place as home? But her friend had lived out here for years; going back to England now must seem just as strange to her, Grace thought.

'I do miss my husband,' Mrs Johnson confessed, 'but at least while I'm still here you can count on me if you need any help.' She smiled as Grace dismissed the servant with a word of Urdu and said, 'However, you seem to be managing quite well, my dear. I feared you might have been sitting here indulging in homesickness and unwilling to do anything, but it seems you are made of sterner stuff.'

'I do have moments when I feel desperately lonely and homesick,' Grace admitted. 'But it does no good to sit around feeling sorry for myself. It's true I can't wait to return to England and I'm thankful we are not staying out here permanently. Nevertheless while I'm here I shall simply have to try and make the best of things.'

'That's the spirit.' Mrs Johnson took a sip of her tea. 'No word from your husband yet?'

Grace shook her head.

'I don't understand him — going off and leaving you all alone like this.' Her friend banged the cup down in its saucer with some force. 'He's an absolute cad, as my husband would say.'

'At this moment I must say that I agree,' Grace replied with a wry smile.

They were silent for a few moments, each woman deep in thought. Grace was about to ask if Mrs Johnson wanted more tea when the older woman nervously cleared her throat, looking almost embarrassed.

'What is it?' Grace asked.

'Has anyone called on you since you arrived?'

'No.'

'And no one has left their card?'

Grace shook her head.

Mrs Johnson sighed heavily. 'I thought not. Usually, when people newly arrive from England, everyone is curious. It's refreshing to see a new face and they can't wait to find out all about the newcomers.'

'So why has no one been?' Grace waited for the reply with a sinking heart; she felt sure it had something to do with the hints her friend had dropped previously.

'I suppose I ought to tell you.' Mrs Johnson hesitated. 'You remember the couple we met at the hotel?'

Grace nodded, her stomach fluttering with apprehension.

'Mrs Wilmot is an avid gossipmonger and she couldn't wait to tell me what she had found out about Mr Eastwood. It's not a pretty story, my dear. Are you sure you want to hear it?'

'I'm bound to find out some time,' Grace said, nodding at her friend to go on.

'Your husband is not all he seems,' Mrs Johnson said.

'So it's true then — he came by his fortune dishonestly — but how did he get away with it? And why come back here where he could be caught and arrested?'

'It's not just that. He ... ' Mrs Johnson paused, her expression embarrassed.

Grace's heart began to thump. What could be worse than stealing? 'Go on,' she said.

Stumbling over her words, stopping frequently to reassure Grace that whatever her husband had done, she could still count on her friendship, Mrs Johnson unfolded the sorry tale.

It was true that Thomas was the son of a British colonel in the Indian army — but his mother was a Hindu.

'Such liaisons are nominally frowned on but if the couple marry . . . ' Mrs Johnson paused. 'Thomas was sent to school in England. Despite his dark colouring he was accepted there as a European. I don't think you suspected, did you?'

Grace wasn't as shocked by this as her friend clearly expected her to be. She was more concerned about the accusations of dishonesty. But there was more . . .

Mrs Johnson cleared her throat. 'Now, I cannot vouch for the truth of this but Mrs Wilmot seems sure enough. It seems he too took up with an Indian woman and there was a child . . . '

Grace was shocked now. A child? How could he have abandoned it and returned to England to live the life of a gentleman, deceiving her parents into believing he was of the gentry and a fit suitor for their only daughter? And he had presented himself as a rich man too — those riches gained dishonestly, if her friend was to be believed.

'But why come back? That's what I can't understand.'

'I think I can guess. His mother and . . . ' she paused delicately, ' . . . the other woman live up in the north. He probably didn't anticipate you coming into contact with anyone who had known him before.'

'You mean he risked arrest to come back and see them?' Grace couldn't bring herself to say who 'they' were.

'You must have heard about the mutiny, the siege of Lucknow? That's where his mother lived. My guess is that when the news reached England he felt he had to come back and make sure they were safe.'

'So, he's not such a cad after all then?'

'True, it seems that he does have some finer feelings,' Mrs Johnson reluctantly agreed.

Although she thought she understood, Grace still didn't know why he'd brought her with him.

'Perhaps he wanted to present a respectable front to society. Being seen with such an obviously suitable wife would have allayed any potential gossip about him.'

That seemed to make sense to Grace and explained why he'd been keen to get married so quickly. No wonder he had been so offhand with her on board ship, worried as he must have been about his 'other family'. Then encountering someone who'd known him in his previous life must have put him on edge in case she learned of his deception. She would never forgive him, she thought now. When he returned, if he ever did, she would tell him in no uncertain terms that she no longer considered herself his wife and insist that he make arrangements for her to return to England as soon as possible.

Tears of anger threatened to choke her and Mrs Johnson, mistaking the cause, patted her hand sympathetically. 'I'm sure things will work out all right eventually, my dear. After all, Mr Eastwood asked you to marry him before he made plans to come back here, so he must at least have been sincere in his feelings for you.'

At one time Grace would have agreed, but given his behaviour on their so-called honeymoon, she was no longer sure.

Mrs Johnson went on, 'As for the suspicion of embezzlement, Mrs Wilmot was probably exaggerating. Nothing has been proved. Once you are home, all this can be put behind you.' She stood up, preparing to leave. 'I'll call again before I leave Calcutta,' she said.

Grace, still reeling from her friend's revelations, wasn't sure what to believe. 'Thank you for coming and telling me what people are saying,' she said as they made their farewells.

'So long as you don't think it was just gossip,' her friend replied. 'I really felt it better you should know. At least now, if anyone you meet acts a little strangely, you'll be prepared.'

'I still find it hard to believe — in fact I won't really believe it until I've tackled Thomas about it,' Grace said.

'I don't advise it, my dear. Things will be easier between you if you pretend ignorance.'

'Perhaps,' she murmured as her friend gestured to the driver of the cart to move away.

After she'd gone, Grace went over the conversation in her mind. Although Mrs Johnson had insisted she did believe her husband had done nothing wrong, she couldn't help remembering that overheard conversation on board ship — as well as the malicious gleam in Mrs Wilmot's eyes.

* * *

Adam had taken to deep sea diving as if born to it and, as well as the satisfaction of doing a job he enjoyed, he was making more money than he'd ever thought possible. After their successful salvage of the French ship, he and Mick O'Brien had been entrusted with several dives off the Kent coast and Mr Deane had hinted that there was a big job in the offing with a fortune waiting to be lifted from the ocean bottom.

Adam's share of the last lot of salvage money had swelled the amount he had saved in the past few months. Even after giving his mother a good portion of it, there was plenty left. He wanted to give her all of it but she refused.

'Save some for the future, son,' she said. 'Who knows how long this run of luck will last?'

Adam tried to tell her there was more work to come but she'd become wary of the fickleness of a living earned from the sea.

'Well, if you need more, you know where it is,' he told her, indicating the tin box hidden under his bed.

'That's yours, son. You'll need it if you get married one day.'

He just smiled but his heart was sad. He didn't think he'd ever marry now. No one could hold a candle to his sweet Gracie. And what was the use of amassing wealth if he had no one to share it with?

Of course, he was pleased to be able to help his mother who had struggled in poverty these past few years. Now she'd been able to give up doing other people's washing and could devote herself to caring for her husband. Her hands, which had gradually lost their rough redness, now looked more like those of the woman she had been in their more affluent days, but sadly the careworn look on her lined face, the sadness in her eyes, could not be alleviated by money alone.

Each time Adam came home he could see the change in his father too. The rise of their fortunes had done nothing to cheer him. Since the accident, when he had been forced to become dependent on his wife and young son, Abel had become more and more depressed. He felt the loss of his independence keenly, his inability to support his family a slur on his manhood.

He had become more withdrawn over the years, his manner surly, his few remarks bitter. Nothing Sarah or Adam could do or say could lift him out of it. And as time passed, his hatred of the Brownlows grew out of all proportion to the perceived wrong they had done him.

Adam still felt bitter too and from time to time that bitterness extended even to Grace. How could she have married and gone off to India without a word so soon after they had declared their feelings for each other? And after he'd saved her life too? Despite knowing that her father would never have allowed her to marry a Crossley, he had always nurtured the faint hope that one day things might come right for them. Now, it was too late.

Lost in thought, he jumped when Sarah spoke again. 'Will you be going away again soon, Adam?'

'I expect so. I'm waiting to hear about our next job.' He took his mother's hand. 'I'll be home for a while anyway. You do understand that I need to travel where the work is, don't you?'

'Of course, it's just that . . . ' she nodded towards the chair in the corner where Abel was dozing fitfully, his breath coming in short gasps.

Adam squeezed her hand. 'I know you worry about him but he's been like this for months.' He tried to reassure her but he could offer little comfort. He could tell that his father was becoming weaker.

Sarah's voice caught on a sob. 'I

couldn't bear it if you were away and anything happened.'

*   *   *

When he went down to the beach the following day Adam was pleased that the boat wasn't yet ready. It had been drawn up onto the foreshore on their return from their last trip so that the barnacles could be scraped from the bottom. As soon as the job was done they would be off on another salvage trip.

How could he leave his mother to cope with Abel's worsening condition — but how could he let Mr Deane and Mick down?

It was true he'd made enough money to keep his parents in relative comfort until another job came along, but he wanted more than that. It wasn't enough that his mother no longer had to take in washing, that they could afford the medicine to alleviate his father's pain. He dreamt of moving

160

them from the tiny damp cottage to a house up on the hills above the town — a house with piped water, even a bathroom and inside toilet.

And deep down, scarcely acknowledged, was the thought that one day he could prove himself to be as good as the Brownlows even if it was too late for him and Grace.

Deep in thought as he crunched over the shingle towards the yard where Mr Deane's boat was laid up, he was startled when a deep voice called out, 'Back from your travels, Crossley?'

He looked up to see James Brownlow lounging against an upturned boat. He was tempted to ignore his former friend but James went on. 'Must be a bit of a comedown working for someone else after you've owned your own business.'

The familiar sneer was back and Adam felt a powerful urge to smash his fist into James's face. He curled his fingers, digging his nails into his palm and replied, 'It's honest work — not like some I could mention.' He hadn't meant to taunt the other man but the effort of keeping his suspicions to himself was almost too powerful to ignore.

'What do you mean?' James asked indignantly.

'Whatever you think I mean,' Adam replied, turning away. He hunched his shoulders, expecting a blow.

James merely laughed. 'Good luck to you. I hear this diving business is really dangerous. You could end up dead — or crippled like your father.'

Adam whirled round, almost giving in to his earlier impulse to hit the other man. He was saved by the intervention of Mick O'Brien who hailed him from the deck of the boat which was propped up on stilts on the sloping beach.

'Hey, Adam, come and give us a hand.'

Adam's fists dropped to his sides and he walked away. James's voice followed him. 'You haven't asked after my sister, Crossley. I'm pleased to tell you she's made a good marriage and is enjoying

162

her new life. We've just had a letter saying they arrived safely in Calcutta.'

So that was that; he might as well put Grace out of his mind forever, Adam thought. With a determined effort he put both his former sweetheart and the encounter with James out of his mind and tried to concentrate on getting the boat ready for its next salvage operation. He didn't care how dangerous the job might be. What did he have to live for anyway?

Then the thought of his mother's careworn face and his father's pain-filled eyes struck a chord of remorse. He owed it to them — and to his mates on the diving team — to do the job to the best of his ability. He could not let them down.

8

When Mrs Johnson arrived to fulfil her earlier promise to take her shopping, Grace didn't really want to go. She had counted the money Thomas had left for her to pay the servants and buy food and it was dwindling alarmingly. She was reluctant to spend more, not knowing how long she'd have to make it last.

She tried to refuse but Mrs Johnson insisted. 'You need to get out of the house,' she said. 'I know you are anxious about Mr Eastwood but it does no good to sit here brooding.'

Grace wasn't sure what to expect from their shopping trip. She had only caught glimpses of the noisy bazaars with their colourful array of Indian goods on her arrival in the city. Her eyes widened when the cart pulled up in front of Taylor's Emporium and she was even more amazed when they went inside.

Mrs Johnson smiled indulgently. 'You look like a child in a sweetshop,' she said.

Grace laughed. 'That's what it feels like!'

She looked up at the display of chandeliers suspended from the ceiling, taking in the classical columns that divided the aisles crammed with tables laden with elegant china, table lamps and pictures.

And all around them were the European shoppers, the ladies in fashionable dresses and elaborate bonnets, the men in army uniform or smart coats and breeches. Standing against the columns the scantily-clad Bengalis awaited orders. Grace realised that most of them were not just there to buy goods but to meet and socialise with their friends. Mrs Johnson did not stop to speak but exchanged nods and smiles with several of her acquaintances.

She stopped in front of one of the

tables which contained a beautifully-decorated dinner-service, the plates and dishes edged with gold, not unlike the one Grace's parents owned.

'What about this one, my dear?' her friend asked.

Grace shook her head. 'I don't think it's worth buying anything just for the short time I'll be here,' she said, reluctant and too embarrassed to confess that she was short of money.

Mrs Johnson seemed to guess at the reason for her hesitation. 'Just put it on your husband's account,' she said. 'That's what I do.'

Grace wasn't even sure if Thomas had an account at Taylor's and dreaded the embarrassment she would suffer if she was refused credit. 'No, really, Mrs Johnson. I won't buy anything today. If it seems we will be staying longer I'll think about it.'

Her friend did not press the matter but led her on to the next display. The goods on offer were all of good quality and Grace would have loved to buy a few things to make the bungalow a little more homelike, but she resisted the temptation, taking pleasure in helping Mrs Johnson to choose some things for herself instead.

After arranging for the goods to be delivered, Mrs Johnson suggested they go to the hotel for tiffin. As she did not relish the idea of going back to the lonely house, Grace agreed, although she dreaded meeting any of her friend's acquaintances. Fortunately there was no sign of Mrs Wilmot but Grace noticed that, although several people nodded to Mrs Johnson, they did not stop to chat or ask to be introduced to her companion.

'I see the rumour mill's been in action,' Mrs Johnson said.

'What do you mean?' Grace asked nervously.

'Those old cats in the corner — see how they've got their heads together. No doubt they've found out who you are.'

'But how . . . ?'

'As I told you, Grace, gossip is the main currency out here. Take no notice of them; they can't harm you, especially as you will not be staying in Calcutta for long. And those ladies will be leaving the city soon, too.'

Grace made a determined effort to ignore the covert glances that were thrown their way and tried to enjoy the unaccustomed outing. When Mrs Johnson had left to join her husband, she would be all alone and she didn't think she'd have the courage to venture into the city again.

On her return to the bungalow the now familiar feelings of depression settled over Grace again and she paced the sparse rooms restlessly, wondering what Thomas was up to and what she would say to him when he finally deigned to turn up.

Mrs Johnson called on her twice more before her friends arrived to escort her on her journey up country and Grace felt bereft at losing her only friend. Anxious as she was to rejoin her husband, she told Grace how bad she felt at deserting her.

'I really wish I could stay longer, my dear, but I must be on my way before the rains come — travelling is almost impossible during the monsoon season — but I hate to think of you coping all alone.' She tightened her lips disapprovingly. 'Oh, that husband of yours. I could — '

'I'm sure he'll be back soon,' Grace interrupted.

'Well, don't forget — if you need any help at all, don't hesitate to contact Mr Leeson at Government House. He knows of your situation and will be able to advise you.'

'I'm sure I shall be just fine,' Grace replied.

She wasn't sure she liked the idea of Mrs Johnson telling a stranger about her problems but she knew her friend meant well. Besides, she told herself, Thomas would be back soon and there would be no need for her to see this Mr Leeson, or anyone else for that matter.

She smiled and thanked Mrs Johnson for all her help and, promising to keep in touch, she waved her off, biting back tears as the cart disappeared round the corner.

She had tried to sound confident but inside she was shaking. How would she cope? There had been no word at all from Thomas and, despite her continuing anger with him, she longed for him to return if only for the sight of a familiar face and the company of someone who knew how things were done here.

Apart from the loneliness and the strangeness of her surroundings, she had another worry to contend with. Thomas had assured her that the money he'd left would be sufficient for her needs until he returned, but it had almost gone and she had none of her own to pay the servants with, or to buy food. She could only pray that he would not be delayed much longer.

She wandered round the bungalow, biting her nails and trying to make up her mind what to do. She was missing Mrs Johnson already. If only she had someone to talk to, but her only companions were the servants who, although anxious to please, were hardly likely to be able to help in her present situation.

She couldn't help smiling at the thought of trying to communicate her concerns to Ranjit or the mali and she gave herself a mental shake. Much as she dreaded the thought of having to confide her troubles to a stranger, she decided that rather than feeling sorry for herself she would ask Ranjit to arrange transport for her into the city.

I'll go tomorrow if Thomas isn't back, she thought.

Having made the decision, she felt better and decided to go for a walk in the garden. The air was much fresher today with a light breeze, hailing the cool season that Thomas had promised when they arrived in Calcutta. So far it had been so hot and humid that she had begun to think he'd been merely trying to reassure her.

She strolled through the garden, inhaling the heady scent of the tropical vines. Would she ever get used to the strangeness?

An unexpectedly sudden lump clogged her throat as she remembered walking in the woods above her home town. How she longed for the sight of blue-bells and primroses, the delicate perfume of the wood violets.

It was all too much and she rushed back to the bungalow and threw herself down on the bed, sobbing. At times like this she almost felt life wasn't worth living. Was it for this that Adam had pulled her out of the harbour that day?

*　*　*

She must have slept for hours, she thought, waking to darkness and a loud drumming on the roof. She sat up, wondering why the servants had not come in to light the lamps. As she fumbled for the little clock she kept on the bedside table, the drumming on the roof grew louder.

'It's rain,' she said aloud. The monsoon that Mrs Johnson had predicted had arrived and by the sound of things was in full spate. She got up and went onto the veranda, her eyes widening at the sight of the water streaming over the edge of the roof like a continuous waterfall. Peering through the curtain of rain she saw that the beaten earth of the compound beyond the house was already a sea of mud. Even the worst storms back home had not prepared her for this.

She returned to the house and met Ranjit who looked relieved to see her. 'You are well, memsahib?' he asked. 'I came in when you were sleeping but did not wish to disturb you.'

She assured him that she was perfectly all right and asked him to fetch her some tea. He gave a small bow and withdrew quietly. That was another thing she couldn't get used to — the way the servants came into the room without knocking and could appear so suddenly and silently.

While she waited for the tea, she sat on the veranda looking out at the continuous rain, marvelling at its intensity. Despite it being much cooler it was still very warm and she had no need of a shawl as the day drew to a close. At home she would have been shivering, driven to go indoors and sit by a roaring log fire.

She wondered what they might be doing now, back at The Towers. It was June so, if it was a fine evening, they might be sitting in the garden, looking down the slopes towards the sea and the red sails of the fishing and oyster boats as they made their way back to the harbour.

The mental picture brought another pang of homesickness, but this time she refused to give into it. She'd done enough crying for one day.

Tomorrow, if her husband still hadn't turned up, she would simply have to take matters into her own hands and try to sort out her own problems.

She fingered the brilliant sapphire ring that Thomas had given her. At least she had something to sell if she ran out of money. There must be a dealer in second-hand jewels somewhere in this huge city. And, she reminded herself, there was the ruby necklace too. That should fetch a good price. The jewellery held no sentimental value for her, after all — not like the pearl brooch, which, despite Thomas's protests, she still wore every day.

Nothing would induce her to sell that, she thought, even if she were starving.

Surely the sale of her necklace and ring would raise enough to pay her passage back to England? For she had finally made up her mind that if, as it appeared, her husband had actually deserted her, she would find a way to get home by herself, somehow or other.

★ ★ ★

Three days later it was still raining. Ranjit told her it was dangerous to go into the city while the monsoon raged, but she insisted. Having decided to call on Mr Leeson and to try and sell her jewellery, she would not be thwarted.

Anish accompanied her, holding an umbrella over her head which did little to keep her dry. When they reached the gates she saw that the road in front of the bungalow was now a raging river. She gazed transfixed as leaves and branches swept past, jumping back in horror as a dead dog bumped against the fence.

'Please, memsahib, go back to the house,' Anish implored.

Swallowing hard, she complied. She would have to wait for the rain to stop. One thing was certain — there was no hope of Thomas returning while the monsoon continued. She would just have to manage for the time being.

Still determined that, with or without her husband, she would seek passage on a ship returning to England, she filled in the time sorting out her possessions and packing them into the tin trunk which had accompanied her on the outward journey.

To her dismay, she found that many of her dresses were already spotted with mildew due to the pervading damp, and she threw them aside, selecting the least damaged to pack. Perhaps the metal trunk would keep them dry. She was glad of it, having already learnt that anything made of wood was soon eaten by termites. Her few books were already unreadable, chewed to pieces by insects.

She sat back on her heels, wondering at her naivety. How different to her imaginings her life had turned out. What had happened to her sense of adventure, her determination to enjoy the experience of a strange country? Now, all she wanted was the cool wind off the North Sea, the cry of the ever present gulls fighting for scraps of fish, the smell of tar and sawn wood as she walked along the shore with the sea on one hand and the busy boatyards on the other.

She bit back the tears which threatened. She would not be defeated; it must stop raining some time. The rivers would turn to roads again and she could carry out her plan. She would allow nothing to stop her from going home.

★ ★ ★

It seemed to have been raining for ever when one morning it stopped — quite suddenly, as if a tap in the sky had been turned off — and then a pale sun appeared, turning the drops on the leaves to diamonds.

Grace turned to Ranjit, who was clearing away the evening meal. 'I'll be able to go into the city now, won't I?' she said with a hopeful smile.

He shook his head. 'It will rain again soon, memsahib.'

'Surely not. I can't believe where all this water comes from.'

'The rains last for many days. Sometimes it stops for an hour, maybe two, but it will return. I do not think you should try to leave the bungalow. I have heard that the river has flooded part of the town. Many stalls in the bazaar have been swept away, people's homes too.'

'What will happen to the people?' Grace asked.

Ranjit shrugged casually. 'They will build again when the waters go down.'

Grace was genuinely appalled. 'Does this happen every year?' she asked.

'Always the rain, but not always the floods. This year it is bad, the worst for many years.'

Grace's thoughts turned to Mrs Johnson and she hoped that her friend had managed to reach her home in safety. Thomas, too. However angry she was with him, nevertheless she did not wish him any harm.

Ranjit could not give an estimate as to how long the rains would last and Grace resigned herself to waiting patiently until the water subsided and she could go into the city. She did not expect to see her husband any time soon. Even if he was on his way back to Calcutta by now, the floods would prevent him travelling any further. She had no way of knowing how badly the rest of the country was affected but it was probably worse out in the country-side.

She decided to make the most of the brief respite from the downpour and went outside. The bungalow was built on slightly higher ground and had escaped the flood, but the garden sloped down towards what passed for a road and it was a sea of mud. As she gazed at what had once been a mass of tropical blooms, the heavens opened and in minutes it was as if the sunny spell had never been.

As Grace turned to go back into the house she saw a movement down near the gate. She peered through the misty rain, wondering who it was. Probably one of the servants had taken advantage of the lull in the storm to go to the market in search of provisions, she thought. But, as the figure came towards her, she gasped in surprise — it was Thomas!

His clothes were crumpled as if he'd slept in them and his face was flushed, his eyes feverish. He was carrying a large leather holdall bag which she did not recall seeing before. She hurried towards him as he stumbled up the veranda steps and tried to take it from him.

'Here, let me,' she said.

Even as he almost collapsed at her feet, he clung on to it. 'Just let me get inside, out of this rain,' he said.

She took his arm and helped him up the steps, calling for Ranjit as she did so.

He sank into the nearest chair and looked up at her as if he'd only just noticed her. 'Thank God you're still here,' he gasped.

'Where else would I be?' She couldn't help the sharp retort which left her lips before she had time to think.

He didn't seem to hear. 'Grace, please . . . ' His voice trailed away and he closed his eyes.

Grace shook him. 'Thomas are you ill?'

He didn't reply. Gently, she disengaged his hand from the heavy bag and set it down in a corner of the room just as Ranjit appeared. The servant took in the situation at once and clapped his hands to summon the other servants. Together they carried Thomas into the bedroom and laid him on the bed. His clothes were soaked and streaked with mud, his hair and beard tangled.

'Whatever happened to you?' Grace asked as she gently helped him out of his clothes, but he shook his head and mumbled something she could not hear.

Ranjit ordered one of the boys to heat water for the sahib's bath and another to bring tea.

Thomas opened his eyes. 'No tea . . . whisky.'

The servant poured a measure and handed it to him, steadying it as the glass rattled against Thomas's teeth.

Two of the boys carried the tin bath into the room while another brought cans of hot water. Thomas was too weak to climb into it and Grace sent the servants away. Using the hot water they'd brought, she gently sponged the mud from his face, then combed his hair, removing the tangles.

He submitted to her ministrations but avoided her eyes when she asked again where he'd been and what had happened to him. When she persisted, he pushed her away and closed his eyes. She sighed and stood up. Perhaps she should let him rest. It was obvious he was far from well and, whatever Mrs Johnson had told her, she still couldn't quite believe that her husband was the cad she had hinted at.

She would wait until he was feeling better and then tackle him. She definitely wasn't going to pretend that everything was all right between them;

she had a right to know what he'd been up to, she told herself.

As she stood up to leave the room, he began to thrash around in the bed, mumbling to himself. She leaned over him . . . what was he saying?

'What is it, Thomas?' she asked.

He didn't appear to hear her but continued muttering, his face contorted with grief. 'Dead, they're all dead!' he cried.

Alarmed, Grace grabbed his arm and shook it. 'Who?' Had he seen people swept away in the flood?

He twisted away from her and she laid a hand on his forehead, hoping to calm him but she snatched it away quickly. His skin was burning with fever.

'Ranjit!' she called. 'We need a doctor — quickly!'

'I will send Anish,' he said, 'but I do not know if he will be able to reach him.'

'You must try. Mr Eastwood is very sick,' she fretted.

She turned back to the bed and began to bathe Thomas's forehead with the now cool water. It might help to bring the fever down, she thought.

She felt helpless, never having had to deal with serious illness in her life and with little idea what to do. It did not occur to her that he might be contagious; her natural instinct was to do what she could to help.

★　★　★

When the doctor arrived he took one look at Thomas and shook his head.

'Is he dying? He can't be!' Grace cried, guilt flooding her mind. She had been ready to believe what people were saying about him without giving him the chance to explain. Now she found herself praying that he would recover.

The doctor finished his examination and straightened up. 'Try to keep him cool and give him plenty of water — boiled first, mind.' He closed his bag and made to leave.

'Will he get better?'

The doctor smiled sadly. 'It's too soon to tell. The fever may break. We'll know in a day or two. I'll come back tomorrow.'

When he'd gone, Grace returned to the bedroom and sat bathing Thomas's forehead and trying to get him to take sips of water. For most of the time he seemed comatose but now and then he would thrash his head from side to side, muttering.

Occasionally she was able to make out a few words but he was speaking mostly in Urdu. The only English words were 'dead' and 'bag'. Perhaps he wanted something from the bag he'd brought home with him, but she was reluctant to leave his side to go and look.

Much later Ranjit entered and told her he'd prepared food, but she shook her head and sent him away.

She sat for what seemed like hours as day turned to night and still the rain drummed on the roof and a smell of dampness pervaded the house. The thoughts whirled in her head as she went over everything Mrs Johnson had told her.

She still found it hard to believe that Thomas had deceived her, but how could she complain when in effect she had deceived him too? Hadn't she accepted his proposal of marriage while still in love with someone else?

The thought of Adam knifed through her and she cursed the older generations of their two families. How could they let a matter of business come between them and make it impossible for her and Adam to ever find happiness together?

Weariness overcame her and her eyes were beginning to close when she was jerked awake by her husband's voice. He spoke more clearly than before, repeating the phrase, 'Dead, they're all dead.'

'Who do you mean, Thomas?' Grace asked.

'Mother, Anuradha, the baby . . . I

was too late . . . ' he muttered, as tears began to course down his face. 'Grace, forgive me,' he muttered.

Grace took his hand and squeezed it but words would not come. So it was true then; he did have a child and another woman. Whether he had married this Anuradha or not seemed immaterial at this moment. All Grace knew was that he had deceived her. Her earlier thoughts of forgiveness fled and anger rose in her breast. Why had he done it?

Thomas relapsed into silence again and she sat beside him, still holding his hand through the long night as she tried to think about the future and what she would do if he survived.

Perhaps the other woman had died before her marriage, thus making Thomas a free man and their union legal. Besides, no one back in England need ever know about his past. Could she live with that and try to make a go of things?

Then there was the suspicion of his

criminal activities. Although Mrs Johnson had stressed that nothing had been proved against him, Grace felt that he would not have left the country so abruptly if he had been innocent. He must have loved this other woman very much to risk returning here. That thought did not distress her — it was the deception that did.

All the anger she had repressed rose up to choke her. She had determined to make the best of things, do what her parents thought best for her, and this was how he had treated her.

Adam would never have behaved like that. He had always been honest with her.

'Oh, Adam,' she cried silently. 'Why didn't you ask me to run away with you? I would have followed you anywhere, given up my home and family for you. Did you ever really love me?'

She thought again of the day Adam had saved her from drowning. Why had she let James bully her into keeping quiet about it? If her parents knew what Adam had done they would surely have accepted him as a suitor, and she would not be here now, nursing a man she didn't love, trapped in a strange country with no friends.

Tears began to fall, splashing onto the hand that still held Thomas's and he moved restlessly.

She brushed them away, together with regrets as to what might have been. Whatever Thomas had done, he was her husband, he was sick and he needed her, so for now she would do her best for him and when he was well again, she would make him tell her everything.

Then she would decide whether to stay with him or seek an annulment of their marriage.

9

Adam was on the quayside talking to Mick O'Brien about their latest salvage operation. The wreck in the Solent had yielded several cannons and a couple of anchors which they had sold to the Admiralty. It had been a difficult dive in murky water with strong currents.

Adam had taken it all in his stride, confident with the diving apparatus after so many underwater forays, and Mr Deane now numbered him among his best divers.

He had just told Adam that Mr Deane wanted him on the team for a very important expedition which would take him far from the familiarity of home waters.

'It's a grand opportunity for you son, and the boss wouldn't consider you if he didn't think you could do it,' Mick said.

'I don't want to let Mr Deane down,' Adam replied. 'He's been good to me, but I can't contemplate going to the other side of the world and leaving Ma to cope alone. My father's dying . . . '

'It's up to you son, but you'd be a fool to turn it down. Think what you could do for your family with the extra money. Besides, you wouldn't be much help to them stuck here with no work.'

Adam nodded at the truth of his words but he still wasn't sure. He felt he was being pulled in two. The lure of adventure, almost as much as the lure of money, was hard to resist.

Besides, since Grace's marriage, he longed to get away from the town; wherever he went there were reminders of her and the happy times they'd spent together. But poor Ma, hadn't she had enough trouble in her life without having to look after Dad on her own?

The fishing fleet was making its way into the harbour, the red sails now furled, and he thought of the lean times when there'd been scarcely enough fish to make the trip worthwhile. Could he go back to the uncertainty of that way of life? Mick was right. It wouldn't help Ma or Dad if he wasn't bringing any money in.

'I'll think about it,' he said and walked away, leaving the harbour wall and walking along the shoreline. He passed the boatyard that had belonged to his family, hearing the sound of hammering and men's voices.

The yard was prosperous once more under the ownership of the Brownlows and once again Adam was reminded of happier days. He wondered bitterly what had gone wrong. The Crossleys had been prosperous, too, all those years ago, and then things had started to go downhill; they had lost orders, materials had gone astray. The final straw was the accident that had left his father unable to work.

But had it been an accident? Adam couldn't help wondering, as he had done so often in the years since it had happened.

His memory was becoming a little hazy now, although he had played it over in his mind time and time again. He'd gone to the boatyard after school. The workmen had finished for the day but Abel never went home until he had finished the job he was working on.

As he approached he heard his father's voice raised in anger. Hidden by the stacks of wood in the yard, he couldn't see who Abel was talking to but a few moments later, Charles Brownlow pushed past him. 'Your father's a fool,' he said, striding away across the shingle.

Seconds later, Adam heard a crash and he rushed into the workshop where the piled planks of freshly-sawn wood now lay in an untidy heap. His father was pinned beneath them, unable to move, his face contorted with pain.

'Help! Somebody. Help!' Adam had shouted, straining to lift the heavy planks.

A dark shadow loomed over him and a voice said, 'What has happened?'

He turned to see James Brownlow. 'I don't know — the stack collapsed on him. Help me lift it, James, please.'

Together they had strained to move the heavy baulks of timber pinning Abel to the ground. It was impossible. 'You'll have to go for help,' Adam said, unwilling to leave his father.

As James stood up one of the workmen appeared. 'What's going on?' he shouted in alarm.

'It's Dad, he's hurt,' Adam gasped. 'Give us a hand, Jim.'

Together, the three men had managed to free Abel who by then had almost lost consciousness. When they finally saw the extent of his injuries, James had offered to fetch his father with the pony trap.

Crouching alongside Abel, Adam had gripped his hand. 'How did it happen?' he asked, knowing how careful his father had always been about safety in the yard. Surely he hadn't tried to lift one of the planks on his own.

Abel managed to get a few words

out. 'Brownlow had just left — I turned round — this lot fell on me — ' He gasped with pain. 'Couldn't move — out of the way — quick enough.'

'What made them fall?'

Abel shook his head, groaning with the effort. His eyes closed and he lapsed into unconsciousness.

While Adam had waited for James he looked around carefully, trying to work out what had caused the accident, but he could see nothing to account for it, and slowly a suspicion wormed its way into his mind. How had James Brownlow appeared so opportunely — had he been here all the time? Worse, had he pushed the pile of wood over? But why would he want to kill or injure Abel Crossley?

Adam hadn't wanted to believe his former friend was capable of such an act, but slowly, over the years, the suspicion had grown to a certainty and his resentment and hatred had grown.

The accident, if that was what it was, had led to the Crossleys losing their business and the Brownlows becoming richer than ever. Adam couldn't prove anything though, and after all this time he had begun to realise that it did no good to let it continue to fester. Now that he had the chance to recoup their fortunes, he must finally accept what had happened and try to let go of the bitterness that had soured him for so long. At least he could make life easier for his mother, even if, as he dreaded, his father might not live to see it.

He hurried through the back streets to break the news to his parents that he was joining the next salvage expedition and that he might be away for many months.

Even as he reached the end of the alley that gave on to the row of cottages, he knew something was wrong. A group of neighbours clustered in the courtyard and from inside the cottage he could hear the sound of weeping. He rushed inside and flung his arms round his mother, trying to comfort her.

They had both known the end was

near but neither had expected it to be so sudden. He hadn't even had time to say goodbye.

★   ★   ★

Grace nursed Thomas for almost a week. During that time she hardly ate or slept, ignoring Ranjit's entreaties for her to take care of herself in case she should become ill too. During that time, her husband became more and more delirious, muttering to himself incessantly, sometimes shouting and even trying to get up.

'I should have stayed, faced the music,' he muttered during one period of lucidity. 'It was wrong of me to leave them.'

Grace couldn't have agreed more but she tried to comfort him. Time enough for recriminations when he was well again, she thought.

A little later he mumbled her name but she couldn't make out his next words.

She leaned closer. 'What is it, Thomas?'

But his head tossed from side to side, his eyes wild. 'I wanted to be respected . . . to be a gentleman,' he said. 'Foolish, I was so foolish . . . '

Through the long days and nights of his delirium, Grace gradually pieced the story together. It was clear that he had truly loved Anuradha and was proud of his little son, but when it seemed certain that his embezzlement of company funds was about to be exposed, he had left his family and fled to England, taking with him most of his ill-gotten gains.

He had sent his wife back to her home village, promising to return for them later, but he had no intention of coming back, wishing to spare them the shame of association with his crimes.

Back in England he'd adopted the pose of an English gentleman, choosing to settle in the small Kent coastal town where he could be reasonably sure of anonymity. It was when news of the

Mutiny reached England that he began to fear for his wife and child and he determined to go back and get them to safety, but he was too late. They were all dead — Anuradha, his child, his mother. Tears rolled down his flushed cheeks as he recalled what had happened to them.

'But why did you have to marry me — and why insist on me coming with you?' Grace asked, bewildered, almost choking on the words.

Thomas looked at her, his eyes clear for the first time since his return. 'I needed a wife of good family — I wanted to be respectable, accepted . . . ' he said, turning his head away in shame. 'I'm sorry.'

Grace stood up abruptly and left the room. How could he have done this to her? Her fists clenched in anger, then relaxed as she acknowledged she had treated him badly too, marrying without love, knowing her heart belonged to Adam.

She went onto the veranda, scarcely

noticing that the incessant rain had finally eased until a sudden shaft of sunshine dazzled her. Tears pricked her eyes and she told herself it was the bright sun that had caused them. In her heart she was crying for herself and Adam, but some of her tears were for Thomas and his lost family. He had behaved badly, it was true, but in a way she could understand his actions.

Still, whatever he had done, she was his wife — his true wife, for she had worked out that Anuradha must have died before her wedding. She didn't really care for herself, but she knew her mother would take comfort from the fact that a scandal could be averted. Perhaps her parents need never know the full story of Thomas's marriage, or that he had been suspected of embezzlement. For, with time to think, she had decided to stand by him. After all, what choice did she really have?

The idea of being married to a criminal bothered her a little but she salved her conscience with the thought that the money could be used to do good when they got back home — that is, if they managed to get away from Calcutta before the authorities caught up with Thomas. She was sure that the Wilmots, as well as the man she had seen on the ship, would have passed on the news that he was back in India.

Hopeful that he was beginning to recover, Grace was impatient now to make arrangements for their passage home.

She returned to the bedroom, determined to tell him of her decision to if not to forgive, then at least to stand by him. He had seemed so lucid a few moments ago and she was sure that his fever must have broken and that he was on the road to recovery.

As she approached the bed, she realised she was wrong.

He was so still that at first she thought he was sleeping peacefully, but as she reached out to smooth his hair, her smile turned to a grimace of horror. Her cries brought Ranjit and the other servants running as she sank to her knees beside the bed, sobbing uncontrollably.

10

Grace woke once more to the sound of rain drumming on the roof and she buried her face in the pillow. Would this monsoon ever end?

It was a week since the funeral and the following days had passed in a blur.

Her cries on discovering that Thomas was dead had brought the servants running and Ranjit, with his usual efficiency had taken control of the situation. He had sent for the doctor to sign the death certificate as well as for the English priest.

The incessant rain had turned the grounds around the bungalow into a lake and they had difficulty getting there, but to Grace's relief when they did arrive some hours later, they took matters out of her hands.

In this climate the funeral had to be held quickly, the doctor explained. 'Is there anyone who can stay with you, to help make the arrangements?' he asked.

Grace shook her head. The only person she knew out here was Mrs Johnson who had left Calcutta before the start of the monsoon season.

'Never mind. Leave everything to me,' he said, patting her hand gently.

After the service at St James's Church, the hearse, followed by Grace and the doctor in his own carriage, splashed through roads which had almost turned to rivers. The servants followed on foot. They reached Park Street Cemetery with its huge mausoleums looming through the curtain of rain. But Grace scarcely noticed her surroundings as she stood at the graveside with Ranjit holding a huge black umbrella over her head.

Now as she woke once more to incessant rain, she realised that she couldn't stay shut up in the bungalow for ever. It was time to make decisions and the first thing she must do was to pay the servants. She did not deserve their loyalty, she thought. Ranjit in particular had been most solicitous, bringing her food and drink and urging her to eat.

Mrs Johnson had been wrong; none of the servants had tried to take advantage of her distress and ignorance of the customs of the country. In fact they had done all they could to help and make her feel at home and she realised how fortunate she was.

She couldn't expect them to carry on looking after her with no pay and the few coins she had found in Thomas's wallet were long gone, most of it used to pay the doctor. She had tried to ask him about money but he had been too ill to respond. It was time to take matters into her own hands.

Thomas's bag, which he had dropped in the corner on his arrival, was still there, untouched since his collapse. She picked it up and emptied it on to the bed. Despite its heaviness, all it contained was soiled clothes and she sighed in disappointment.

Thomas's empty wallet lay on the bedside table with his gold pocket watch. She picked it up, wondering how much she could sell it for. Perhaps it would buy food for a few days, she thought, but she would need more than that to buy her passage home.

She crossed to the bureau where her jewel box stood and took out the ruby necklace. Tugging her engagement ring off her finger, she strode to the door and called for Ranjit.

He appeared almost at once, smiling when he saw that she was up. 'Memsahib is feeling better?' he asked. 'Perhaps you will eat something now.'

'Later,' she said, holding out the jewellery and the gold watch. 'Ranjit, I need your help. I wish to sell these. Do you know how I might go about it?'

'No, memsahib; no. You must not. The betrothal ring — I know it means something to your people. And the rubies — a gift from your husband.' He shook his head. 'No, you cannot.'

The jewellery, even the engagement

207

ring, held no sentimental value for Grace but she could not tell the servant that. 'I need money. You and Jamal, Anish and the others . . . you have not been paid . . . '

'That does not matter, memsahib. We will look after you.'

Tears welled up at his kindness and she smiled. 'I cannot allow that,' she said. 'You must be paid. Besides, there is nothing to keep me here in Calcutta. I must have money to return to England.'

Ranjit nodded and gave a small bow. 'I understand, memsahib. I will make inquiries.'

'Thank you.'

The servant smiled. 'Now, memsahib — you will eat?'

'Yes. I'll try anyway.' She didn't think she would be able to swallow anything but she realised she must try. She had scarcely eaten in the days since Thomas's death and she had noticed that her clothing was beginning to feel loose. She needed to keep her strength up if she was to manage her own life from now on.

She spent the next few days sorting out her possessions and deciding what to take with her on the voyage home. The few books she had brought with her were half-eaten by termites and the damp humid air had spotted her dresses with mildew. If Ranjit got a good price for her jewellery perhaps she could buy new clothes before she left.

The thought made her pause. Ranjit had taken the watch and her ring and necklace, saying he might not be able to find a buyer straight away, but it had been several days now and he had not mentioned it since. Had she been wrong to trust him? Perhaps she should have taken Mrs Johnson's advice and sought out Mr Leeson at Government House.

* * *

The East Indiaman was anchored out in the bay, its sails furled while the equipment for the dive was loaded onto it from the small boats which had rowed out from the harbour. Much as he hated leaving his mother alone since the death of his father, Adam could hardly contain his excitement at the start of this, his first long sea voyage.

Of course it wasn't the voyage itself or the prospect of diving for real treasure that had set his heart hammering when he learned of their destination. India! He couldn't believe it. The very place where Grace now was. And Mr Deane had picked him for the job.

'Whereabouts in India?' he asked.

'We'll be diving down to a ship on the River Hooghly. Seems it was wrecked on a sandbank,' his employer replied.

The name meant nothing to Adam, his knowledge of geography was hazy. All he knew was that India was a big country and his shoulders slumped as he realised his chances of running across Grace were very slim.

'Is that anywhere near Calcutta?' he asked hopefully, a big grin splitting his face as Mr Deane nodded that it was. James Brownlow had told him they'd received a letter from Grace and mentioned Calcutta.

'The city is a few miles up-river — there's a harbour there — but we'll be working nearer the mouth of the river,' Mr Deane said. Seeing Adam's disappointed look, he laughed. 'Don't worry, you'll get a chance to see the sights.'

'Thank you, sir,' Adam said. He walked away, hugging to himself the thought that he might be lucky enough to encounter Grace and see for himself that she was all right. If she seemed happy with her husband and her new life then he would try to put thoughts of her out of his mind and make a new life for himself.

Then his shoulders slumped as a new thought occurred to him. He knew that the ship Grace and her husband had sailed on was destined for Calcutta, but was that the Eastwoods' final destination? They could have travelled onwards and now be anywhere in that vast country.

He thought about swallowing his pride and asking James Brownlow for news of his sister, but James probably wouldn't tell him anyway. Adam had bitten his lip in frustration, at the same time acknowledging that he should not be thinking of Grace now that she was married. The truth was that not a day went by when he did not think of her. There was always some small thing to remind him of the precious times they had spent together — a glorious sunset, the sight of the little turnstones looking for food among the pebbles on the beach.

As the last of the cargo was loaded and Adam joined the rest of the diving team on board, he couldn't help a little spurt of optimism. The despair he had felt at the thought of Grace being on the other side of the world lifted a little. Every day that passed from now on would bring him a little nearer to her.

Once he arrived in India he would make enquiries. If he could only have news of her, discover that she was well and happy in her new life, he would be content — or so he told himself.

When everything was stowed away to Mr Deane's satisfaction, Adam and Mick went up on deck and leaned on the rail. As the great sails went up to the shouts of the sailors swarming in the rigging and the great ship began its stately passage out into the North Sea, Mick waved a hand back at the receding shore.

'Well, we're off. Let's hope the next time we come up this estuary we'll be rich men,' he said.

Adam smiled and nodded but, despite his excitement at the coming voyage, he felt a small pang at leaving home for so long. He had been away before — to Portsmouth which had seemed a million miles away at the time, and to France — but India . . .

Who knew how many months would pass before he saw his mother again?

He had left the proceeds of his last dive for her to pay the rent and other living expenses. He could sail away with a clear conscience, knowing she was financially secure — and then there was the prospect of making his fortune and being able to make life easier for her when he returned.

He turned his face to the wind and watched as the bow of the ship ploughed its way through the waves. There was no turning back now.

'Mr Deane was lucky to get passage on this ship. We'll get there much faster than the ordinary passenger ships,' Mick said, interrupting Adam's thoughts. 'Lucky too, that there was space in the hold for our diving equipment.'

The East Indiamen carried tea and other goods to the Port of London from China and India, only stopping briefly at Cape Town before sailing on into the Indian Ocean. With luck and good weather they would reach the mouth of the Hooghly River in a matter of weeks. And further up the river lay Calcutta and the prospect of news of Grace.

11

Grace was relieved when, a few days after handing over Thomas's watch and her jewellery, Ranjit approached her with a hesitant smile. He must have sold them then.

Her relief turned to apprehension when he spread his hands and shrugged his shoulders. 'I am sorry, memsahib. I wish I could have got more.' He withdrew a small leather bag from the folds of his robe and handed it to her.

Her heart sank when she tipped the coins out on to the table and saw how little money there was. She had hardly got used to thinking in rupees instead of pounds but she could tell at a glance that, although there was enough for food and to pay the servants, there was not enough to pay for a passage home.

She covered her face with her hands. What was she going to do? Ranjit coughed softly. 'I am truly sorry, memsahib. I did my best. The man who bought them was suspicious — he almost accused me of stealing. I didn't want any trouble so I accepted his offer without haggling.'

She had a fleeting suspicion that he might have cheated her, but the sorrowful expression in his liquid brown eyes told her he was telling the truth. Besides what did he have to gain? It was his wages and food that the money was to be used for. 'You did the right thing, Ranjit. Thank you,' she said, smiling.

Despite the knowledge that the sale of her jewellery had bought her a brief respite from hunger and destitution, a feeling of panic assailed her. She couldn't stay here for ever. The bungalow was rented and the lease would run out soon and she had no means of earning money. Who could she turn to?

She became aware that Ranjit was speaking. 'I hope you will forgive me, memsahib. I gave some of the money to Jamal to buy food. He will be back soon and the cook will prepare a meal for you.'

'Thank you, Ranjit, but I can't eat,' Grace said.

'You must. I cannot let my memsahib fall ill.' He gave his sad smile, bowed and left.

Grace scooped up the coins and put them back in the leather bag. She paced the room, listening to the rain and almost giving way to the impulse to scream for it to stop. She couldn't think for the noise.

She went into her bedroom, lay down and closed her eyes, but the sound of water pouring down from the eaves and gurgling its way across the sodden compound kept her awake.

Suddenly she sat up. This would not do. She was behaving like a child, expecting someone else to solve her problems when she would simply have to sort things out herself.

Grace remembered her friend's advice

to go to Government House if she was in trouble. She didn't care if it was still raining tomorrow; she would wade through the floods on foot if necessary. It was time she took matters into her own hands and got on with her life.

Standing up, she went to the tin trunk where she had begun to keep her clothes since the start of the rains. Even locked away here they were beginning to smell of the damp that pervaded the house. She must find something suitable to wear for her visit to Government House. She pawed through the silk dresses, the chemises and petticoats with little enthusiasm, remembering how excited she had been shopping for her trousseau in London with Mother.

Now it seemed as if all that had happened to another person. She wondered what Mother would think if she could see her now with all her high hopes for her daughter in tatters.

Grace held up a gown of yellow silk. This one seemed to have escaped the pervading spots of mildew and she laid it on the bed. It would do for tomorrow. She spotted the leather money bag on the bedside cabinet. She would need some money to pay the driver — that's if she could find someone willing to take her by cart into the city.

She took some of the money and transferred it to her reticule, looking round for somewhere safe to put the rest of it. Thomas's bag was still in the corner of the room where she had thrown it after emptying out the soiled clothing which had all been burnt after his death for fear of transferring the infection.

She picked up the bag, deciding to pack some of her personal belongings in it. She would hide the remaining money in with them until it was needed.

As she put the bag on the bed she realised it still seemed quite heavy. She had thought it was empty. As she pulled the handles apart to look inside, a loud hiss made her rear back. A small scream escaped her lips as a thin yellow snake slithered out onto the bed.

'Ranjit, come quickly!' she shouted.

The boy, Jamal, came running in. 'Ranjit is not here,' he said. 'What is it, memsahib?'

Wordlessly she pointed to the snake which was now curled up on the pillow, occasionally raising its head and hissing.

Jamal laughed and picked it up, holding it firmly behind its head. 'No harm, memsahib. It is good luck snake.' He grinned, showing his white teeth.

Grace shuddered. 'Take it away . . . please,' she begged.

He opened door onto the veranda and threw the offending reptile out into the compound where it quickly wriggled away under a bush.

Still grinning, the boy left the room and Grace sank down on the bed, holding her hand over her heart to still its panicked beating. How could such a vile creature bring good luck, she thought crossly, but as her heartbeat slowed and she regained her composure, she recalled the beautiful brilliant colours and markings on the snake's body and inwardly berated herself for her panicky reaction.

Grace told herself that she was right to be wary; some snakes were poisonous, not to mention spiders and scorpions and other deadly insects. On that thought she picked up Thomas's bag and turned it upside down, shaking it vigorously.

Something rattled and she almost dropped it. There was something else inside. Cautiously, she put her hand in, feeling around. The piece of board that stiffened the bottom was loose and she eased it out and felt around, trying not to think of snakes and spiders. Beneath the board she discovered a hidden compartment containing several small leather bags, similar to the one Ranjit had brought the money in.

She picked one up and opened the drawstring, tipping it up and spilling a glittering fountain of gold coins onto the bed.

Her eyes wide, Grace emptied each of the bags — one contained emeralds, the others sapphires, rubies and diamonds. She scooped them up and let them trickle through her fingers in a rainbow shower, laughing out loud. Here was enough to pay the servants, to let them eat well, to buy new clothes for the voyage home — and best of all, to pay her passage home. She was rich!

The euphoria lasted only a moment and her laughter faded. How had Thomas come by this wealth? Not honestly, she was sure, given the rumours she had heard. What should she do?

Hastily, she thrust the coins and jewels back into the bag, sure that the treasure was not hers to spend. It must be part of the fortune Thomas had supposedly embezzled from his employers, and she suppressed a sudden sneaking suspicion that perhaps his real reason for returning to India had not been to ensure the safety of his wife and child but to retrieve the bag of gold and gems.

* ★ ★

When Grace woke the next day she lay for some minutes listening to the unaccustomed silence — a silence broken by the voices of the cook and his boy arguing in their own language in the kitchen behind the house. It took a moment for her to realise why their voices sounded so clear — the rain had stopped.

She sat up and pulled the muslin net surrounding the bed aside. Was this really the end of the monsoon season or just a brief respite from the relentless rain as had happened several times before? A bar of sunlight filtered between the shutters and lay across the floor and Grace smiled, thinking it a good omen for her meeting with the man at Government House. Perhaps the snake had been lucky after all.

She hastily pulled on a wrap and pulled back the shutters, stepping out onto the veranda into hot sunshine. Curls of steam rose from the sodden ground, wreathing the battered flowers and shrubs in mist.

It really did seem that at last the rain had stopped and she prayed that the clouds would not roll in again, bringing even heavier downpours than before.

She looked up into a brilliant blue sky — not a cloud in sight. Surely at last the monsoon season must really be over. Her relief was quickly replaced by the thought that now would come the cloying sticky heat and that would be just as hard to cope with as the rain. She couldn't bear to stay here any longer; she must make her plans without delay.

As she dressed she pondered what to do about the wealth of coins and precious gems she had found stashed away in the hidden compartment of Thomas's bag. The temptation to keep them hidden and say nothing was very strong, but her innate honesty overcame her need for funds to finance her voyage home and she quickly suppressed the tiny flicker of avariciousness. She decided to keep the gems hidden for the time being and to ask the advice of Mrs Johnson's friend.

Now that she was able to make plans for her future, Grace felt much better and was even able to eat the meal that Ranjit set before her. He smiled approvingly when he came to get his orders for the day and saw the empty dishes.

'Ranjit, are the roads clear yet? I need to go into the city today,' she said.

He shook his head. 'The waters are going down, memsahib, but you should wait a day or two.'

'No, I can't wait. I must go today.' Grace knew that another day would make no difference but now she had decided on a course of action, she couldn't bear any delay.

Ranjit bowed and said, 'As you wish,

memsahib. I will send Jamal to fetch a cart.'

Grace thanked him and retired to her room to get ready, wishing there was some other mode of transport than the cumbersome, noisy bullock carts.

On her arrival in Calcutta she had seen a few carriages such as were common at home, as well as people riding high on the backs of elephants. Well, she couldn't afford a carriage and the idea of climbing onto the back of one of those huge beasts was more terrifying than exciting.

A cart it would have to be. Besides, the cumbersome vehicle would be more suited to driving safely over the rough, flood-damaged roads.

By the time she was dressed, the cart and its driver were waiting at the foot of the veranda steps. Ranjit helped her up onto the seat and Jamal jumped up behind. She didn't really need anyone to accompany her but Ranjit said he'd feel better if she had one of the boys with her. He wasn't happy about her going into the city alone.

The driver flicked his whip over the backs of the bullocks and the cart moved off slowly through the gates and out onto the road which was still slick with mud brought down from the hills.

It was rapidly drying though and the heat was already intense. The boy held the bright pink and green parasol over Grace's head and she was grateful for the shade.

As they approached the city it grew noisier. The road was lined with stalls, the merchants shouting their wares, holding up brightly coloured lengths of silk. Grace wrinkled her nose at the smell of spices mixed with dung although by now she had almost become accustomed to it.

She averted her eyes from the beggars lining the roadside, holding out their stick thin arms in a plea for alms. She wished she had something to give them, although when she had first arrived Mrs Johnson had discouraged her.

Now, she was almost a beggar herself, she thought. At least it seemed that way when she considered that she would be asking Mr Leeson for help to get her home again. She was convinced that the gold coins and jewels had been stolen and that she would be forced to give them up. Perhaps the government official would be able to help her trace the rightful owner of them all.

The cart left the teeming streets and turned into Chowringhee, the street of shops and government buildings. At the end of the wide avenue, set back from the road among well-tended grounds, Grace caught a glimpse of a large white building with imposing columns, gleaming in the fierce sun. The driver halted the cart in front of the main entrance and Jamal helped her to descend, still holding the parasol over her head.

The entrance was flanked by two Indians in white, their heads swathed in heavy turbans. They stood to attention and did not change their expressions as

Grace hesitantly approached. Should she just go straight in? She glanced behind her but the cart with its driver and the servant were already disappearing round a corner.

She walked up to the door which was opened from within and found herself face to face with a dark-complexioned man in European dress.

'What can I do for you, madam?' he asked in excellent English, his musical voice betraying his Indian-origins.

'I wish to see Mr Leeson,' Grace said, hoping she did not sound as nervous as she felt.

'I will see if he is available. Please wait here,' the man said, leading her to an ante-room furnished in European style with comfortable arm chairs and small tables on which were several magazines and newspapers.

Grace looked around her with interest, admiring the ornate furnishings and sparkling chandeliers. After the spartan conditions of the bungalow, where it seemed she had lived for ever, it seemed incredibly luxurious.

The minutes dragged on and Grace picked up one of the newspapers. It was a three month old copy of the Times and, although she did not usually bother with the news when she was at home, she devoured the words, home-sickness overcoming her as she read of what had been happening in that far off country she called home. Even a report of the Prime Minister's speech in Parliament, which normally she would have dismissed as boring, was read avidly.

Immersed in the paper, she did not notice the soft-footed approach of the servant who came to conduct her to Mr Leeson's office.

The man who stood up to greet her was red-faced with a huge moustache, his nose purple from too much alcohol and Grace took an instinctive dislike to him, but when he smiled kindly and offered her tea, she relaxed a little. After all, she told herself, first impressions could be deceiving as she well knew from her experiences with Thomas. Mrs Johnson would not have recommended him if she thought he would be unwilling to help.

She accepted the offer of tea and sat in the chair he indicated while he rang the bell for a servant. He waited until the tea was brought and poured and the servant had left before leaning forward and asking why she was here.

Hesitantly, Grace mentioned her friendship with Mrs Johnson whom she had met on the voyage out. 'She told me if I were in trouble, I should contact you,' she said, blushing a little.

'And are you in trouble, Mrs Eastwood?' he asked.

She thought she detected a slight emphasis on the word 'Mrs' and wondered if he knew about Thomas's other wife. She was reluctant to continue but he smiled encouragingly.

'My husband died,' she said, choking a little on the words.

Mr Leeson made a sympathetic sound and nodded at her to go on.

Gradually she poured it all out — Thomas leaving her alone to go and visit his mother, her fear that he had deserted her, having to sell her jewellery to pay the servants. She did not mention her discovery that he had already been married when he proposed to her and that he had a child. Since learning that they had died she did not think it affected her status as Thomas's wife and, if he did not know of it already, why divulge such a shameful thing to a stranger?

'You mean to tell me that Mr Eastwood has left you destitute?' Leeson asked.

'He said he would have more money on his return to Calcutta, when he had completed his business,' Grace said. 'He did not tell me what his business was though, but he was a rich man — at least my parents thought so when we first met.'

Mr Leeson leaned forward. 'You are sure your husband left nothing, made no provision for you in the event of his death? Surely there was a will of some sort. Did you find nothing among his personal effects?' He rapped out the questions while his eyes bored into her.

Grace flinched. Despite his seeming friendliness at first, he now seemed quite hostile. The feeling that she could not really trust him crept up on her and she decided not to reveal what she had found in Thomas's bag. All she wanted from Mr Leeson now was information about booking a passage back to England.

However he continued to question her, insisting that Thomas must have left a will. 'Are you sure you've searched thoroughly?' he asked. 'And what about his bank — have you inquired there?'

Did he know about the gold — but how could he? 'I don't know where he banked — he did not tell me anything about his business,' she said, shaking her head vehemently.

He patted her hand. 'Never mind, my dear,' he said, the friendly smile back in place. 'Well, as you have no relative or friend here to speak up for you, would you like me to make inquiries for you at the bank?'

'Thank you, that is most kind,' Grace said, making an effort to be polite. She couldn't wait to get away from the man, but he was her only hope. 'I just need enough money to pay my passage home. My parents will take care of me once I reach England again safely.'

He stood up to indicate that the interview was at an end. 'Leave everything to me, Mrs Eastwood. I will call on you in a day or two and let you know what the situation is.'

★　★　★

Back at the bungalow Grace could not settle to anything. Her belongings were packed and she had told Ranjit that she was making plans to return to England. When he had expressed regret and wished her well, she realised she had become fond of the little man in the weeks she had been here. He and Jamal were the only thing she would miss about India though.

As the days passed, the heat increased and Grace grew more and more impatient to be gone, but there was no message from Mr Leeson and she began to think that he had no intention of helping her. Surely it did not take this long to inquire at the bank about her husband's finances and to let her know if there was any money due to her.

Perhaps she should have confided in him about the hidden wealth beneath her bed? After all, she had no intention of keeping it and would be delighted if it could be returned to its rightful owner. It wasn't as if she had stolen it herself.

Then she remembered the look on the government official's face, his eyes boring into hers as he relentlessly questioned her. She suspected that he knew all about her husband's misdeeds, but how could he know that Thomas had returned from his travels up country with a bag of treasure? Worse, did he suspect her of being his accomplice — was he even at this moment planning to have her arrested?

She paced the veranda, flicking the fly whisk in agitation. The insects were becoming more numerous with the increasing heat, but it wasn't the flies that were bothering her.

Ranjit came out with a tray containing a jug of lemonade and Grace threw herself down on one of the rattan chairs. One of the boys ran up and squatted behind her chair, pulling on the punkah in an effort to create a cooling breeze.

As she sipped her drink and looked out over the garden, which was beginning to recover from its battering by the rain, she thought that if only things had been different she might have enjoyed her stay in this country, but she would always long for home, she thought, remembering the red-sailed boats dotting the curve of the bay, the mingled smells of freshly-sawn wood and tar in her father's boatyard — and Adam, who had saved her life so many months ago.

Once more she berated herself for not standing up to James and braving her parents' displeasure at her disobedience. Perhaps knowing that Adam had rescued her from drowning would have softened her father's attitude to him and helped to mend the relationship between the two families. Perhaps it wasn't too late, she thought, now that she was no longer bound by the duty she had owed to her husband.

Grace allowed herself to picture Adam in the familiar surroundings of their home town. What was he doing at this moment? Was he at sea on the *Emma Jane* with the Smythes, or helping to unload a collier in the harbour? Or had he left the town and joined the navy, as he had threatened to do? He was a hard worker, she knew, and would do all he could to support his parents and make their lives a little easier.

The store of gold and gems hidden in the room behind her forced its way into her head. If it were hers she could do so much good with it — not just for Adam and his parents but for some of the poorer people in her home town. She was sorely tempted to keep it.

12

At the very moment that Grace was sitting on her veranda on the outskirts of Calcutta day-dreaming of Adam, he was leaning over the ship's rail drinking in the sights that had so enthralled her all those months ago.

Ever since they had sighted land his stomach had been churning at the realisation that he was nearing the country where his loved one was. As the ship rounded the southern tip of India and sailed into the Bay of Bengal he had begun to realise just how vast the country was. It would be several days before they had made their way up river to the port of Calcutta and he did not even know if Grace was there.

He had been told that most of the British moved up into the hills at the start of the hot weather. His common-sense told him that she was unlikely to still be in the city and, even if she was, the chances of seeing her was very slim indeed. He consoled himself with the thought that at least he might be able to get some news of her.

He would be content if he could simply make sure she was well and happy — at least that was what he told himself — but she had not been out of his thoughts since they had set sail and more than once Mick had teased him about the faraway expression in his eyes.

'Dreaming of some lassie, are you?' he asked.

Adam had denied it several times but, under his friend's relentless teasing, he had confessed that there was a 'lassie' who had stolen his heart. When he told Mick that she had married someone else, his friend laughed.

'Well, stop mooning after her, mate,' he said, clapping Adam on the shoulder. 'There's plenty of other girls who'd love a well set up lad like yourself.'

Adam had to admit his friend was

right. He had met several of them on his travels — some of them not the sort of girls his mother would approve of, but none of them — even the respectable ones — could compare to his Gracie.

Still, he told himself, as the ship heaved in sight of the harbour at Calcutta, perhaps it was time to stop making himself miserable over something he could do nothing about. He promised himself that, if he discovered that Grace had settled into her new life with Thomas Eastwood and seemed content, he would try to forget her. He doubted if he would ever find another girl to match up with her though.

Their arrival in Calcutta had been delayed by the monsoon and the captain had apologised for their slow passage up the Hooghly. The great river, which in the dry season was a smooth slow-moving body of water, was now a roiling mass, carrying with it whole trees and other debris, including the bodies of dead cattle. How on earth were they going to find the wreck, let alone salvage it, Adam wondered.

Mr Deane sought out the members of the diving team who were clustered on deck impatiently waiting for the ship to dock. 'The captain tells me that many of the sandbanks have shifted over the past few months. I've been assured that things will settle down now that the rains have stopped, but our job will be more difficult now — the wreck may have shifted too. We'll have to do a preliminary survey before we can start diving,' he said.

Adam prayed that Mr Deane would not need him for the survey. He had hoped to have some time in the city before starting work on the dive. More chance of finding out about Gracie, he thought.

But first, there was work to do.

After the weeks of inactivity on board ship, Adam was pleased to be busy. Even so, as they unloaded the diving equipment onto the quayside, he couldn't help stopping every now and then to gaze around at the unfamiliar sights. He was used to the noise and bustle of ports, having worked in Portsmouth and Southampton, as well as visiting the Port of London on diving business.

Here there were the same warehouses, the same frantic activity, but Calcutta was nothing like he'd imagined. He thrilled to the sights and sounds — the colourful and varied costumes, the babble of foreign languages and the unusual smells — not all of them pleasant.

Recalling Grace's adventurous spirit when they were children he smiled at the thought of her wonderment when she would have arrived here several months ago. She would have loved the colours the women wore, the spicy fragrances, all telling of a vastly different world from the one they had grown up in.

If only they could have experienced it together, he thought wistfully, his eyes misting over.

A shout from behind him broke his reverie and he ducked as a bale being loaded onto the ship swung past him.

'Come on, mate!' Mick called. 'Stop daydreaming and help me get this stuff onto the cart.'

Adam apologised and joined the other men. The diving equipment was to be taken by cart to a small dock at the other end of the harbour where a boat was waiting to take them back down the river to the site of the wreck.

By the time they had re-loaded everything, the sweat was pouring down Adam's back and his shirt was sticking to him. He watched the native Bengalis in their loincloths, envying their seeming indifference to the cloying heat and the freedom of movement their sparse clothing gave them.

To his relief, Mr Deane dismissed the men, saying that lodgings had been found for them at a house near the harbour.

'I'll just take a couple of men in the morning to see if we can locate the wreck,' he said, gesturing to two of the other divers.

He turned to Adam and, to his relief, said, 'We won't be needing you until the diving starts. Why don't you and the rest of the lads take the opportunity of seeing the sights? We'll all meet up at the lodging house tomorrow evening.'

Once they were satisfied that all was prepared and ready they all retired to their lodgings.

After a meal consisting of unfamiliar spiced meat and flat round pieces of a kind of bread, the men were more than ready for bed after their exertions of the afternoon.

Adam fell into bed, exhausted, but found he was unable to get to sleep for excitement. Maybe tomorrow he would finally find out if Grace was still in Calcutta — he might even be able to see her if he was very lucky. He tried not to think about how he might feel if he did, however.

★　★　★

Mr Leeson still had not contacted her and Grace was becoming really concerned. She had given Ranjit the last of the money she'd got for her jewellery the day before and he had replenished their food supplies, but she knew that what was in the store cupboard would not last long.

What would she do if the food ran out before the man from Government House got in touch?

Grace sighed. She would have to go into the city again but she did not even have enough coins in her purse to pay for a cart and driver and she didn't fancy the walk in this heat.

I'll wait a couple of days, she thought, *and then if I don't hear from Mr Leeson, I'll send a note.*

A few days later there was still no word and Grace reluctantly decided to use one of the gold coins from Thomas's bag to buy food and pay the servants. She retrieved the bag from under the bed and, remembering the snake that had found its way inside, opened it cautiously. Laughing at her own nervousness, she shook a coin out of the smaller bag, feeling slightly guilty as she did so. Surely it wouldn't hurt to take just one. She could pay it back if necessary once she got back to England.

She then scribbled a note to Mr Leeson and called to Ranjit. He came in straight away but before she could send him on the errand, he said, 'There is someone to see you, memsahib — a Mr Leeson.'

'Don't show him in yet — I must dress first,' she said, suddenly conscious that she was still in her robe. She had not expected him to call in person, nor so early in the morning before she was properly dressed to receive visitors.

'Very well, memsahib,' Ranjit said, turning to leave the room.

She called him back and pressed the gold coin into his hand. 'Can you use this to buy food?'

His eyes widened but he nodded. 'I will change it for rupees,' he said.

Grace knew she did not have to explain but she felt she had to say something. 'It was in my husband's bag,' she said.

He grinned, showing his white teeth. 'I will spend it wisely, memsahib,' he said.

A noise at the entrance made Grace look round and she gasped as the government official barged into the room. How dare he walk in unannounced! She pulled her robe more closely around her and forced a smile.

'Good morning, Mr Leeson. How kind of you to call.' She did not trouble to disguise the sarcasm in her voice.

He did not smile in return. Instead he grasped Ranjit's arm roughly and snatched the coin from him. 'Where did you get this?' he snapped.

'I gave it to him,' Grace said as firmly as she could muster.

'And where may I ask did you get it, madam?' he asked, whirling to face her. 'I seem to remember you telling me you were all but destitute.'

'I found it in my husband's belongings.' Grace's eyes flicked to the bag which stood open on the table. Should she tell him what it contained?

Before she could speak, his eyes narrowed suspiciously. 'Just the one coin?'

She nodded, suddenly unwilling to trust him.

'Then it seems you really are in need of my help,' he said, his eyes gleaming as he took in her state of undress. 'A woman alone surely needs a protector.'

Grace swallowed hard as she took in his meaning. He was offering to help her in return for — what? She forced a smile. 'You are very kind, sir, but as I explained, I only need my passage home. My father is a rich man and he will take care of me once I'm back in England.'

'I understand,' he said, glancing to where Ranjit still waited by the door. 'Are you going to offer me any refreshment, Mrs Eastwood? It is a hot ride out from the city.'

'Of course. Forgive me.' She gave an order to Ranjit, telling him to hurry; she did not want to be alone with Leeson any longer than necessary.

She turned to him and, forcing a smile, said, 'If you'll excuse me, I must get dressed. Perhaps you will wait on the veranda.'

He nodded, tossing the gold coin up in the air and catching it, all the while raking her body with his hot eyes. 'But may I say, my dear lady, that you look most charming as you are.'

He put the coin in his waistcoat pocket and took a step towards her.

Grace suppressed a shudder and moved away quickly, hurrying into her bedroom and closing the door. The sooner he had his drink and went on his way, the better. She would manage on her own rather than accept anything from him. She dressed quickly, glancing frequently towards the door. His words and actions had given her another reason to no longer trust the man.

She was sitting at her dressing table

pinning up her hair when the door opened and he stood there, smiling that false smile.

She whirled round. 'Mr Leeson, how dare you come in here!'

'Forgive me, Mrs Eastwood. I thought I heard you call,' he said, coming towards her. 'As I said, I am always willing to help a lady in distress. You should not be alone at this sad time.'

'I am not alone. I have my servants.'

'It is not the same. I can help you, if you will let me.' He reached out and touched a strand of her hair.

Grace shrank back in her chair, glancing over her shoulder towards the door. Where was Ranjit? As she opened her mouth to call him, Leeson grasped her shoulder pulling her towards him, laughing as she began to struggle.

'Come, dear lady, surely you do not begrudge your protector a little kiss. It is a small price to pay for my silence.'

'I don't know what you mean!' she gasped, pushing him away as firmly as she could.

'Why, the gold, madam,' he snarled. 'I do not believe there was only one coin in your husband's bag. Where is the rest?'

'Why should I tell you — that is, if there really is more?' Grace was defiant but she realised in an instant that her words were almost an admission that he was right.

'I will find it,' he said. 'And, since you will not be kind to me, I will not return the compliment. I would have kept quiet about it, given you a share, but now, I must inform the authorities.'

'You do not frighten me, Mr Leeson. I think you had better leave now,' Grace said. She practically pushed him out of the door just as Ranjit reappeared with the drinks.

Leeson stepped away from her and moved towards the open french window. 'A pity. I had thought we could be friends.'

Grace just stared at him and his eyes narrowed.

'Well, it is your choice. Just remember that whatever your husband left you when he died, was not his to bequeath.'

Grace looked to where Ranjit still waited by the door, holding the tray. 'Please show the gentleman out,' she said.

He nodded and put the tray down, gesturing to the man from Government House. 'This way, sahib.'

Mr Leeson gave a snort of contempt. 'Well, I'll leave you in the capable hands of your servants,' he said. 'You do realise, of course, that once they realise you have no money they will all run away.'

Grace recovered her composure and straightened her shoulders. 'You are wrong, Mr Leeson,' she said. 'Ranjit and the boys are the most loyal of servants. Now, if you cannot help me, I think you had better leave — but first, give Ranjit the money you took from him.'

He laughed again and Grace's face fell as he patted his waistcoat pocket.

'As I said, it is not really yours, is it?' he taunted. Don't think you've heard the last of this. I shall be back and next time I will have a policeman with me. I know you are hiding something.'

Grace couldn't help her gaze going to the open bag on the table. Mr Leeson caught her glance and took a step towards it. She made a grab for the bag, but he beat her to it. Turning it upside down, he gave a shout of triumph as the leather bags tumbled out.

'I knew it! So that's why Thomas Eastwood came back to India — to retrieve his ill-gotten gains.'

'You have no proof of that,' Grace protested.

'But I do have the authority,' he said, scooping up the bags and putting them back in the larger bag. 'I'll make sure these are returned to the victim of your husband's crime.'

'You can't do that!' Grace said. 'If you can prove to me that they're stolen, I'll willingly give them up, but only then.'

He just laughed and picked up the bag. 'I'm sure you realise, madam, that receiving stolen goods is a crime. Think yourself lucky that I don't have you arrested.'

He turned to leave and Grace ran after him, grasping his sleeve and forcing a tear from her eye. 'Oh, please, sir! Don't leave me with nothing,' she begged. She had quickly realised that standing up to him would do no good, but perhaps he was the sort of man to be swayed by a woman's tears.

She was wrong. He shook her off, laughing.

'Too late, madam. If you had been more amenable, we might have shared the booty.' He strode to the door, the bag in his hand, pausing to throw a few copper coins on the table. 'That should be enough to wire your father and ask him to send money for your passage home. Meantime, let's hope your loyal servants can take care of you.'

By the time he'd gone, Grace was crying in earnest, but they were tears of anger rather than dismay. She had seen the avaricious look on the government official's face and she knew without a shadow of doubt that the contents of the bag would never be restored to their owner. Mr Leeson was just as corrupt as her husband had been.

What could she do now but get in touch with her parents? Father would send the money as soon as possible but she dreaded having to tell him and Mama how wrong they had been about Thomas.

As she impatiently dried her eyes, Ranjit asked gently, 'Are you all right, memsahib?'

She nodded and smiled, unwilling to admit how frightened she'd been.

'He is a bad man,' Ranjit said. 'I did not understand everything he said. Why did you let him take your money?'

'It wasn't mine,' Grace said. She was too upset to explain although she felt he would probably be sympathetic. Besides, it wasn't done to confide in a servant, was it?

She waved him away, but a minute later she called him back. 'How do I send a wire?' she asked, at the same time thinking he probably did not know. She had hardly understood what the man had meant herself, but she seemed to recall hearing that there was a marvellous new way of sending messages called the telegraph. She would probably have to go into the city and find out for herself.

To her surprise Ranjit knew where the telegraph office was and offered to go there himself. 'I do not know how it is done but someone there will be able to advise me. If you write the message down I will go immediately.'

'I would prefer to do it myself,' she said, thinking that while she was there she might find an official who would be more sympathetic to her problems. She would ask for advice at the telegraph office. Nothing would induce her to go to Government House again for fear of running into the odious Mr Leeson.

'If you wish, memsahib. Jamal will accompany you.' Ranjit bowed and left the room.

Grace dreaded the long walk into the city but it had to be done and the sooner the better, before the heat grew too intense. She picked up the coins that Mr Leeson had so carelessly flung down and counted them carefully. She had no idea how much it would cost to send a wire and hoped there was enough. She daren't spend any on transport, just in case, but there might be some money left over to enable her to get a ride home.

She dressed in the lightest garments she could find and called for the boy, Jamal, who came in carrying her parasol.

'Do you know where to go?' she asked.

He nodded. 'Ranjit tell me the way,' he said.

As she descended the steps of the veranda, Ranjit appeared. 'Memsahib, please forgive me — you must not go into the city alone. I beg you to let me go instead.'

'But I will not be alone,' Grace said. 'Do not worry, Ranjit — Jamal will take care of me.' She put her hand on the boy's shoulder and smiled down at him.

'As you wish, memsahib.'

*　*　*

In the past couple of days the deep puddles had dried out and the earth was beginning to bake hard. It was difficult to imagine just how sodden everything had been just a few days ago. At least it was easier to walk now, Grace thought. The roads leading to the city centre were lined with graceful palms and she was glad of the shade. She strode out confidently, the boy trotting along beside her, holding the parasol over her head.

After half an hour the heat began to sap her strength and her pace slowed. She began to understand why the few

Europeans she saw appeared so languid. In this climate it was impossible to hurry anywhere.

She passed Taylor's Emporium where Mrs Johnson had taken her all those weeks ago. Thank goodness she had resisted the temptation to buy anything that day, she thought. As they neared the river and its docklands, she could see the masts and spars of shipping between the warehouses and was reminded painfully of the little harbour at home — and Adam.

Never mind, she told herself sternly, once Father gets the wire, he'll send money and I'll soon be on one of those ships.

She stopped as a group of sailors passed her and disappeared round the corner, her heart leaping at the sound of English voices. Perhaps it was because she had been thinking of Adam that she had almost called out. The tall one with dark curly hair had looked so much like him, but it couldn't be, could it? She put a hand over her heart and tried to catch her breath. Foolish girl, she told herself, walking on.

Lost in thought, she started when Jamal pulled on her sleeve. 'Memsahib, here is the place,' he said.

The telegraph office was crowded, the hubbub incredible. Grace pushed her way through the throng to the long counter and waited for someone to attend to her.

The process was a lot simpler than she had expected although it took her a long time to compose the message to her parents. She had been informed that the cost depended on the number of words so she tried to keep it as brief as possible. Finally she settled on *Thomas dead. No money. Please send fare home.*

Grace counted out her coins and was about to hand them and the slip of paper over the counter when she changed her mind and hastily crossed out the word 'please'. One more coin saved meant staving off destitution a bit longer. To her relief there was money left over to hire a cart back to the bungalow. She asked how long it would take to get a reply and was told it would only be a day or two.

'Come back tomorrow and enquire,' she was told.

She dreaded making the long trek again. Perhaps she would ask Ranjit to go in her stead. Although she left the building feeling a bit happier, she was still worried. Even if Father wired back straight away, she might have to wait weeks before anything came from him. She had no idea how money could be sent here. Perhaps he would come out himself and escort her home, she thought, but remembering how long the voyage to India had taken, she realised her troubles were far from over.

She would have to be very careful with what little money she had from now on and she decided to forgo hiring a cart to take her back to the bungalow. It was much hotter now and she decided to wait until the sun began to go down before starting the long walk back — but where could she wait? She daren't enter the Imperial Hotel, the only place she knew of in the city where a lone European woman might be accepted. She dreaded an encounter with the Wilmots or anyone else who might have known her husband.

Then she remembered passing the Emporium on their way here — she would spend the time there; it was quite acceptable to stroll around looking at the goods without buying anything. It would pass the time until the heat of the day died down and it would at least be a little cooler inside.

As she passed through the entrance she saw a couple of beggars being chased away by the uniformed doormen. A day or two earlier she had imagined how she would feel if she were reduced to such straits. The thought made her more sympathetic and she wished she had something to give them, but she held onto her meagre store of coins. Since sending the wire she felt a little better but she wouldn't be entirely free of worry until she had a berth on a ship bound for England.

She strolled up and down the aisles of the huge store with Jamal trotting along behind her. The store was crowded with Europeans, mostly women intent on spending their husbands' money. Grace felt no envy and even had a little sympathy for what she saw as their empty lives. She avoided their interested glances, hoping that no one would speak to her. Mrs Johnson had introduced her to a few people during her brief stay at the imperial but now she was pleased that she had not pursued their acquaintance. She felt sure that everyone must have heard about her husband by now.

She moved away from a group who seemed to be speculating as to who she was and entered another aisle, occasionally picking up a vase or a china dish and examining it as if she intended to buy. *If Father does come to fetch me home in person, perhaps we can come here and buy a gift to take home for Mama,* she thought.

An English voice from behind her echoed the thought. 'Here, Mick, come and look at this. Pretty, ain't it? I'm thinking of getting this to take home for the missus.'

A soft Irish voice replied. 'Good idea, mate.'

The man behind her coughed. 'Excuse me, ma'am. Would you be kind enough to give me your opinion? I'm looking for a present for my wife.'

Grace turned to face him. 'It's lovely. I'm sure she'll love it.' Her voice trailed away as she caught sight of the third man in the group. She had thought she was dreaming when she caught that brief glimpse earlier, but now she was sure. She put a hand on the table to steady herself as her knees shook and the blood drained from her face.

'Are you all right, ma'am?' the first man asked.

'Watch out, she's going to faint,' the

man called Mick said, taking her arm and easing her into a chair.

Grace sank into it and covered her face with her hands. She couldn't believe it. Surely she must be dreaming. Someone took her hands and murmured her name, but she daren't open her eyes. After a moment she had composed herself and, taking a deep breath, she looked up and saw a pair of sapphire blue eyes gazing into hers — Adam's eyes.

13

Adam's hands gripped Grace's as if they would never let go and she gasped, still not quite able to believe it was really him. What was he doing here? For a moment she had the ridiculous thought that he had heard of her problems and had come to rescue her! He still hadn't said a word but just kept holding on to her hands and gazing into her eyes.

Suddenly she became aware that Jamal had appeared, pushing and shoving at Adam and gabbling in his own language.

Adam shrugged him off. 'Go away, I know this lady,' he said.

The boy ignored him. 'Memsahib, memsahib, you are ill? I will fetch Ranjit.'

'Go away, I told you,' Adam said, baring his teeth.

Grace straightened up and smiled. 'It's all right, Adam,' she said. 'Jamal is my servant. He's only trying to help.'

She turned to the boy. 'I'm all right now. It was just the shock. Mr Crossley is an old friend. Go and wait outside and I'll call if I need you.'

She looked up at Adam's two companions. 'Thank you for your help. I'm fine now. Why don't you finish your shopping and leave Adam and me to talk?'

The two men walked away after clapping Adam on the shoulder and arranging to meet up later.

Adam nodded but still remained crouched in front of her chair, his tight hold on her hands almost painful. It seemed he wasn't about to let her go now that he'd found her and she was happy to stay where she was for the time being.

Grace knew that the love she saw in his eyes was reflected in her own and it was as if the past couple of years had never been — the quarrel, the enmity between their families, her marriage . . . thinking of Thomas she suddenly realised that Adam did not know she was now a widow.

She hesitated, wondering if he had really forgiven her for marrying someone else and going off to the other side of the world without even trying to see him and explain.

She must tell him and she opened her mouth to speak but Adam beat her to it, although he could hardly get the words out.

'I can't believe I've found you, my love!' He stopped abruptly. 'I'm sorry, I shouldn't have said that . . . '

'It's all right, Adam. I understand. Such a lot has happened since I left England.' She pulled her hands away and sat up straighter. 'Thomas is dead,' she said abruptly.

Adam quickly took her hands again. 'Oh, Grace, I'm so sorry. What happened?'

'It's complicated.' She couldn't tell him the whole story here, surrounded by gaping shoppers.

'I want to hear it,' Adam said. 'Is there somewhere private where we can sit and talk?'

'We'll go and have tea at the Imperial Hotel — it's not far from here,' she said, standing up and smoothing her gown. Now that Adam was with her she had no qualms about bumping into the Wilmots or any of the other gossip-mongers Mrs Johnson had warned her about.

* * *

Seated at a secluded table, they gazed silently into each other's eyes, only looking away to give their order. When the waiter had brought the tea and a selection of sweet pastries, Adam nodded encouragingly. 'Go on — tell me what happened.'

The tea grew cold and the pastries remained uneaten as Grace re-lived those dreadful days nursing Thomas until his inevitable death.

'I felt so alone,' she said. 'No one came to the house. If it wasn't for the servants ... ' A sob caught in her throat.

'I had understood the British community here was close. Did no one come to help you?'

Grace shook her head. 'My husband was not well liked,' she said. Even now she could not bring herself to talk about Thomas's criminal activities and how she had become unwittingly involved in them.

'I can't pretend to be sorry he's dead,' Adam confessed. 'But I am sorry you've had to go through all this on your own.' He reached out for her hand. 'At least you are well provided for — that must be a comfort,' he said.

Grace gave a short laugh. 'A comfort — yes.' If only he knew. Before he could ask any more questions, she said, 'Now it's your turn. Tell me what you're doing in India.'

Adam told her about his meeting with John Deane, the famous diver, and how he had learned to dive too. He recounted his adventures salvaging Royal Navy wrecks on the south coast and his trip across to France.

'And now, we're hoping to salvage the cargo of a wreck just down the river from here,' he told her.

'How strange that we should both end up here in India,' Grace said almost wistfully.

'I came close to refusing to come,' Adam confessed and went on to tell her that his father had died just before he left England. 'I hated leaving Ma, but she insisted I came. I just hope she's managing all right.'

'I'm glad you let her persuade you,' Grace said. She wanted to ask if he'd known that she was in India and if that had influenced his decision, but she could not voice the thought. After all, as far as Adam was concerned at the time he left England, she was a married woman.

'I had to come once I knew what the cargo was,' he said, his face alight with excitement. 'If we manage to salvage it we'll all be rich. With the money I can give Ma a better life, move her to a nicer house, away from the damp and draughts. If only Dad was still here to reap the benefit.'

Adam's face was sombre and Grace took his hand. How like him to be thinking of others and not of what such riches might mean to himself, Grace thought.

Now it was time to tell her own story, but it was hard to find the words. Instead she asked, 'What is this valuable cargo?'

'It's a hoard of silver. The ship was on its way upriver bringing payment for a cargo of tea and cotton. There was a storm and it sank. The locals tried to salvage it but later storms caused the sandbanks to shift and she ended up in deeper water.'

'It seems strange though, isn't it? Sending all the way to England for divers.'

'Mr Deane's divers are the best in the

world,' Adam said proudly. 'His brother developed the diving helmet which we use now and it's used all over the globe.'

Grace smiled. Obviously Adam loved his work and was proud to be part of the great diver's team. She was pleased that he had found such a satisfying job and that his bitterness at not being able to carry on the boat building business seemed to have faded.

'Adam, I'm so glad you're here. You'll never know how badly I felt, leaving without even a goodbye . . . '

He took her hand. 'You had little choice. I understand that,' he said. 'I must admit I was hurt that I had to hear of your engagement from your brother. He positively gloated when he told me you were sailing for India, but I do understand.' He squeezed her hand. 'Oh, Gracie, don't cry, please.'

The tears fell faster as the realisation of how much she had hurt him hit home. She would not blame him if he rejected her now. 'I'm so sorry,' she sobbed, fumbling in her bag for a handkerchief and dabbing at her eyes.

Adam signalled to the waiter to bring more tea, giving her time to compose herself.

'It's all right, Grace,' he said when the waiter had come and gone. 'I've had time to think over the past months. I was wrong to tell you I loved you, knowing that we would never be allowed to marry. It was selfish of me anyway to dream that you might give up everything for a poor fisherman.'

'But I would have, you know I would!' she protested, sniffing back a tear.

'And I wouldn't have let you,' Adam declared. 'Having made that decision, how could I blame you for obeying your parents and marrying the man they chose for you?'

'I should have refused,' Grace said. 'You saved my life. If my parents knew what you did that day, they would have let us . . . '

'Didn't you tell them?'

Grace shook her head but before she could explain, someone approached their table. She looked up to see Mr Leeson bearing down on them.

'So Mrs Eastwood, you have found a protector I see,' he said, his loud voice causing heads to turn. 'Quite the adventuress, aren't you?'

She stared at him, her face reddening. How dare he speak to her like that. 'I don't know what you mean,' she protested.

'Grace, who is this man?' Adam demanded.

She was about to tell him when Leeson turned to Adam. 'My name is Leeson. I work at Government House. I've had dealings with this young lady in my official capacity. I must warn you that she has been involved in criminal activity and is in possession of stolen goods. She's lucky not to have been arrested.'

'I don't believe you,' Adam said, turning to Grace. 'Tell me he's lying.'

'I can explain,' she said.

'Oh, I'm sure you can,' Leeson sneered. 'Don't be taken in by her, young man. She'll probably give you the hard luck story about being widowed and left to fend for herself. Has she asked you for money?'

'Of course I haven't!' Grace snapped.

'She will,' Leeson said with a short laugh, before striding away towards the bar.

Adam pushed his chair back and hurried after him, grabbing his sleeve and forcing him to turn round and face him.

Grace couldn't hear what they were saying but she was sure Mr Leeson was elaborating the story of the stolen gems and trying to convince Adam that she had been Thomas's accomplice. She hadn't fully realised how much her rejection of his advances had angered him and this was his way of getting his revenge, but surely Adam wouldn't believe anything he said?

He looked back at her but he did not smile and she had a dreadful feeling that he was taking in everything the other man was saying. Surely he wouldn't condemn her without a hearing, but how could she explain? After all, some of what Mr Leeson had accused her of was true — she had asked for money and she had tried to hide the stolen jewels.

She wanted to go over to them and insist on Adam hearing her side of the story but she couldn't bear the thought of a confrontation in this public place. Instead she stood up and rushed out of the hotel. Jamal was sitting patiently on the ground with the other servants awaiting the whim of their masters. Careless about spending her remaining money, she asked the boy to summon a cart to take her home.

As she climbed up she looked back to see Leeson snapping his fingers at his own servant and shouting an order.

Jamal followed her glance. 'Ranjit says he is a bad man. You should not speak to him.'

Grace agreed. With a bit of luck she

need never see Mr Leeson again — but what of Adam? A sob caught in her throat as she realised she might not see him again either.

He had told her he was taking the boat downriver the next day to start work on the wreck. Should she go back and try to talk to him? Surely he would have followed her if wanted to speak to her. She sighed. Perhaps her father would be here soon to take her home and, once back in England, she might get the chance to talk to Adam and make things right again.

★ ★ ★

Adam refused to let go of Leeson's sleeve until he agreed to sit down again and explain his accusations against Grace. He couldn't believe that she could have changed so much since he'd last seen her.

Leeson ordered whisky and, after taking a liberal swig from his glass, said that Grace had come to him asking for help after Thomas had died. The tale he unfolded was not a pretty story and Adam could hardly believe it. What had happened to the innocent carefree girl he had fallen in love with? It was true she had always been a bit wild, a free spirit kicking against the restrictions imposed by society. It was one of the things he had loved about her.

Since hearing of her marriage he tried to put her out of his mind, realising the futility of continuing to dream about her. He had told himself that, as long as she was happy, he was content.

When he had seen her in that big store shopping for all those lovely things, he'd realised how much better off she was with Thomas Eastwood. He could give her so much more than he had to offer and he had not been able to suppress a surge of jealousy. If only she had waited. He was sure that after this trip he would have been in a position to offer her just as much as Eastwood could.

Learning that he had died had given him a jolt. Sympathy for Grace's loss was far outweighed by the realisation that she was now free. He hoped that when he returned home a rich man, he could once more declare his love and this time it would end in a proposal of marriage — after a suitable interval, of course — but it was much too soon to declare himself at the moment.

As he listened to Leeson's story, Adam managed to conceal his disgust at the crafty gleam in the man's eyes, his nervous licking of his lips, his frequent re-filling of his whisky glass.

His temper rose and his fists clenched. How he would love to wipe that grin off the man's face, but it would do no good to make a scene. He was the stranger here, a poor working man, while Leeson was in a position of authority. It would not help Grace if he was thrown in jail for disturbing the peace.

Still, he could not let Leeson get away with slandering his sweet Grace.

He stood up and, keeping his voice level and firm with a great effort, he said, 'I find it very hard to believe that Mrs Eastwood would get mixed up in such criminal activities. I must admit I do believe it of her husband, but if she is involved, it must have come about unwittingly.'

Leeson began to bluster but Adam interrupted him. 'What you don't know is that I have known Mrs Eastwood since childhood. We grew up together and I know she is simply not capable of acting in the way you suggest.'

A cruel laugh burst forth from Leeson's lips and he made an obscene remark. It was almost the last straw and Adam leaned across the table, his clenched fist stopping within an inch of the man's face. Leeson blanched and held up a hand in defence.

Adam's hand dropped to his side and he took a deep breath. 'I'm warning you, Leeson. If you continue to slander Mrs Eastwood you will have me to deal with.'

Without waiting for a reply he hurried away, pausing only to pay for their drinks. Was it too late to catch up with Grace? He must reassure her that he did not believe one word of that awful man's accusations.

Outside the Imperial Hotel he looked frantically up and down the wide street, standing on his toes to look over the heads of the teeming crowds of both Indians and Europeans, but he could not see a woman in a yellow silk dress holding a pink and green parasol. Several Indian youths still clustered round the entrance of the hotel, waiting for their masters but when he asked if any of them knew Mrs Eastwood he was met with a torrent of foreign words and a vigorous shaking of heads.

★ ★ ★

As the cart reached the corner, Grace turned round, scanning the crowded street in the vain hope that Adam had followed her. But there was no sign of him and she sank back on the hard seat with a sigh. Had she found him only to lose him again?

What dreadful quirk of fate had brought Leeson to the hotel at just the wrong time? Her breath came in short gasps, anger rising to choke her at the effrontery of the man. She dreaded to think what tale he was telling Adam now.

She felt no real guilt at trying to conceal the contents of Thomas's bag. After all, she only had Leeson's word that the gold and jewels were gained dishonestly and, if Thomas were still alive, she would have confronted him about it. But from everything she had been told, she had to believe that her husband really had been a thief. Why else had he been so secretive about his business and the source of his wealth?

However, Grace was equally sure that Mr Leeson, a supposedly respectable government official, was just as corrupt. She had first seen the gleam of greed in his eyes when he had snatched the gold coin from Ranjit. Then, when he had tipped the hoard out on the table he could hardly stop himself from touching it.

Surely, if she had been given the chance to explain, Adam would have taken her word that she had known nothing of it until after Thomas's death.

It was the other insinuation that Grace was more concerned about — the inference that she was the kind of woman to use her wiles to influence someone in authority. It was shame and embarrassment that had made her flee the hotel so precipitously. Now, she regretted her hasty action. As the cart rumbled its way over the sun-baked roads to the bungalow, she desperately tried to convince herself that when she saw Adam again everything would be all right. Surely he would not take the word of a man like Leeson.

She got down from the cart and made her way up the veranda steps, picturing Adam here with her, sitting in the shade sipping cool drinks and making up for all the mistakes of the past.

That was when it occurred to her that, even if he wanted to see her again, he no idea where she lived — and she did not know the name of his ship, or where the site of the wreck was.

14

Adam walked to the corner, thinking that Grace could not have got far. She had only been gone a few minutes but there was still no sign of her. He walked back to the hotel and went in, avoiding the coffee lounge where he had left the government official. It occurred to him that Grace might have been staying here as she had mentioned that her stay in India was intended to be temporary.

On inquiry at the reception desk he was told that there were no guests of that name and he turned away in despair. He must find her again — but how?

He decided that as there was nothing he could do at the moment he would return to his lodgings. Perhaps his boss could advise him. Mr Deane had dealt with the officials out here when making arrangements for the dive, so he might know someone who could help.

When Adam got back, his mates were already there, excitedly talking about the sights they'd seen in the city. Mick looked up with a grin. 'Back already, mate?' he asked. 'Thought you'd be taking the lady out to dinner.'

'No such luck,' Adam said pretending indifference. Usually, he could take a bit of teasing, but today his emotions were too raw and he couldn't bear to be the butt of the other man's attempts at humour.

Mick seemed to sense Adam wasn't in the mood and kept quiet, but the others were not so sensitive. They wanted to know how he'd come to be talking to a beautiful young lady and if he'd had any luck arranging another meeting.

Adam shrugged them off and left the room abruptly. Outside, he walked past the now dark warehouses, pausing when he reached the river. He stood gazing down at the water, reliving every moment of his encounter with Grace from that first awestruck moment when he realised it really was her, to her abrupt departure from the hotel.

Recalling his conversation with Leeson he couldn't help wondering if her flight meant that there was some truth in what the man had told him. Why else would she run away? He felt guilty for even entertaining the thought and told himself that he would give her the benefit of the doubt until they met again and he heard the whole story from her own lips.

Would they ever meet again here in India? He was due to go downriver the following day to start the dive and did not even know if Mr Deane planned for them to return to Calcutta before sailing for England. Even if they did, Grace might have already booked a passage home. It seemed he would have to wait until they were both back in their home town before there was any chance of reconciliation.

★ ★ ★

Back at the bungalow, Ranjit enquired respectfully if the memsahib had managed to complete her business at the telegraph office.

Grace nodded. 'I've sent a wire home. My father should send some money soon,' she said, hoping to reassure him in case he might be worried about his wages.

Jamal followed her indoors. 'The memsahib had tea at the Imperial Hotel,' he announced.

Ranjit looked surprised but he admonished the boy. 'What the memsahib does is not your concern,' he said.

Grace smiled. 'I met an old friend just arrived in Calcutta,' she said. Although there was no need to explain to the servant, she did not want him to think that she could afford to take tea at the hotel but not to pay her servants.

She went to her room and took off the silk dress, folding it carefully into the tin trunk. It was one of the few good dresses she possessed now and she wanted to keep it clean and free from mould to wear on the voyage home — or in case she met Adam again.

Perhaps Father would send enough money to enable her to buy new clothes, or better still come himself to take her home. She had never taken much interest in fashion but she had to admit it would be fun to go shopping in the bazaars.

Why was she thinking about such frivolities after what had happened today? Of course, it was a deliberate attempt to try and take her mind off those last few minutes in Adam's company — his stricken face as that horrible Leeson man had made his dreadful insinuations and she had admitted being in possession of the stolen gems.

Tears began to stream down her face and she sat at her dressing table with her head in her hands, sobbing out her anger and frustration. Leeson had spoilt what should have been one of the happiest days of her life and she hated him for it.

As she sat up and dried her eyes, she recalled the loving look in Adam's eyes when he realised he had found her, that they were really together again. She knew she had not mistaken the joy on his face. Despite everything, he still really loved her.

Grace refused to believe that the foul words of an evil and corrupt man could spoil that love. They would be together one day — they must.

★ ★ ★

With hope in her heart it was easier to bear the seemingly endless days waiting for a reply to her message home. Ranjit had gone to the telegraph office for her several times but there had been no reply.

Had Father even received the wire, Grace wondered. It was such a new thing; who knew if it always worked efficiently? She sat down to write a long letter home. At least that had more chance of reaching its destination, she thought. She would just have to resign herself to staying longer.

Grace could have borne it if she'd had sufficient funds to keep herself, but she had spent the last of the few rupees that Leeson had thrown at her so contemptuously and she was becoming increasingly frantic. She went to the kitchen to check on the stores to find that there was only a little flour left and, hanging from a beam, a few pieces of unidentifiable dried meat which looked to her eyes inedible.

She returned to the main house trying to fight down the panic. She didn't only have herself to feed — the servants depended on her too. Ranjit had impressed on her that he and the others were willing to wait for their wages, which were long overdue, but they all had to eat.

She rummaged once more through every drawer and cupboard, hoping to find something she could sell, even though she knew the search would be fruitless. Hot and frustrated she gave up and went out to the veranda, sinking into a cane chair and almost giving way to tears of despair.

Her thoughts turned to Adam as they so often did and she wondered if he was still exploring the shipwreck downriver. Perhaps he had already returned to England but she refused to believe that he would have done so without seeking her out and giving her a chance to tell her side of the story.

She fingered the little pearl brooch which she had worn every day since Adam had given it to her, despite Thomas's early attempts to get her to discard it. It was more precious to her than all the gifts her husband had showered on her when they married. She had vowed never to part with it but now she could see no alternative. It wouldn't fetch nearly as much as the sapphire ring and ruby necklace, but perhaps it would be enough to stave off hunger for a while.

* * *

Mist was curling up from the river as Adam made his way towards the wooden jetty where the diving boat was moored. After several dives over the past few days they had finally located the wreck and today, they might get lucky and start bringing up the cargo.

This had been one of the hardest dives Adam had attempted so far — and the most dangerous. The waters of the English Channel were cloudy at the best of times but here it was like making your way through thick soup.

The small boat reached the site of the wreck and Adam and Mick donned their diving suits. The dive assistants fixed their helmets in place, checking that the screws were tightened before giving the nod for them to go over the side.

The moment that the water closed over his head was always the worst one for Adam. There was always that niggling doubt that something had been forgotten, that water would fill his helmet or that the hoses would become tangled, but once his heavy boots found the seabed he relaxed.

There was a job to do and he had limited time in which to do it. He could just make out Mick's body alongside his, the wreck looming up in front of them. Using hand signals, they began to move around the hulk, looking for a way into the hold.

Last night in their quarters, the men had eagerly speculated about how much silver they could hope to recover and what they would do with their share of the salvage money. Adam had joined in half-heartedly, consumed with thoughts of Grace — as he had been ever since that miraculous meeting a few days ago.

His mind wasn't on the silver but on how he could find her again. He needed to reassure her that he took no account of what that hateful man had implied. It was unthinkable that the Grace he knew would ever behave in that way.

As he gingerly felt his way around the wreck and stepped through the gaping hole in the hull, he went over that encounter in the hotel, wishing he had gone after Grace straight away instead of staying to listen to that horrible man's insinuations.

His mind was not on his work and he stumbled over a spar that lay across the entrance to the hold. Mick was behind him and grabbed his arm, making a sign to be careful. Adam proceeded more carefully, forcing thoughts of Grace away and concentrating on the job in hand. It would not help her if he had an accident now.

Inside the hold it was even murkier and even with the lamp that was fixed to his belt, he could not see much. Debris swirled around them, disturbed by their passage through the wreck. The dim outlines of fish darted between them. They would have to try to feel their way forward and simply hope to come upon the chests which the ship's owners had told them contained the silver coins and ingots.

Adam's foot bumped against something solid and he looked down — there they were, piled haphazardly now due to the shifting of the wreck in the recent storms. He turned to Mick, giving the thumbs up sign. They had found the cargo!

He tugged on his air line, giving the signal that they were ready to start sending stuff up to the surface. Mick leaned towards him, shoving the face plate of his helmet close so that Adam could see his teeth bared in a grin of triumph. They would be going home rich men.

That would show the Brownlows, Adam thought, seizing one of the chests with renewed vigour.

Mick took the other handle and they carried it out through the hole in the side, tying it to the rope before going back for another. They worked steadily, always conscious that any movement of the cargo might cause the wreck to shift again.

They had sent a dozen chests up before Mick tapped Adam's arm indicating that they had been down long enough. It was time for the other members of the team to take over. He pulled on the line, asking to be hauled up.

★ ★ ★

Back on deck he took a deep breath as one of the men pulled his helmet off. Much as he loved the excitement of the dive, it was a relief to be safely back and breathing fresh air. He kept the rest of his gear on in case he was sent down again, although he didn't think there'd be time for another dive today.

He sat in the shade of tarpaulin, eating the food they had brought with them. He relaxed, gazing across the rolling river towards the distant city, hazy in the heat. After a while he half-dozed, lulled by the musical voices of the Indian crew as they loaded and stacked the money chests.

He was awakened by the sound of the divers returning and he stood up, gazing in awe at the number of boxes piled on the deck. Surely there couldn't be many more still down there.

Mr Deane called to him, pointing towards the north, where dark clouds were massing. The monsoon might be officially over but it looked as if there was another storm on the way.

'Joe says there's only a few more chests,' the boss said. 'You and Mick better fetch them up. It might be too late tomorrow if those clouds are anything to go by.'

Now that he was familiar with the wreck, Adam found the entrance to the hold without difficulty and he and Mick made their way to where the remaining chests lay. The debris stirred up by the divers' movements was swirling around them and Adam began to feel a little uneasy. Was it just the movement of the flotsam in the water or was the ship itself moving?

He reached out to tap Mick on the

shoulder, wondering if he had noticed it too. As he did so, the ground shifted beneath his feet and he lurched sideways. Suddenly, heavy baulks of timber crashed around him he frantically tugged on his line, giving the distress signal.

15

Twice more Grace had sent one of the boys to the telegraph office to enquire if there was a reply from her father. He had returned shaking his head and she was becoming impatient.

She decided to go herself this time and called for Ranjit. 'I will take Jamal with me,' she said.

He protested as she had known he would, but she was firm. She had very little money left now and hesitated to hire transport, but even the long hot walk in to the city was preferable to hanging around the bungalow, bored and frustrated. Perhaps she would try to sell the pearl brooch while she was there.

She pinned it to her bodice, swallowing a lump in her throat at the thought of parting with it; she had promised to wear it always, and even during her short marriage, she had kept her promise — but she and Ranjit and the others must eat.

Grace went out to the veranda where Jamal waited with her parasol already unfurled. It was still early in the morning and not yet too hot to walk but it would not be long before the heat became intolerable. Yesterday there had been more rain — a sudden brief storm which had helped to cool the air a little but only for a while. Grace had been fearful that the monsoon had returned but Ranjit reassured her.

'The rains are over, memsahib,' he said. 'There will be no more rain now for many months.'

The roads were bone dry already and signs of the recent floods were gradually disappearing. As they neared the main streets they passed market stalls where a week previously there had been only a sea of mud. The people bustled around, cheerfully shouting their wares in that medley of languages that Grace was becoming used to hearing. She marvelled at how quickly they had recovered.

When they reached the telegraph office she asked Jamal to wait while she went inside. To her relief, the man behind the counter smiled broadly in response to her enquiry. 'Wire for Mrs Eastwood? Yes, memsahib.'

He handed the slip of paper over the counter and she scanned the few words quickly, sighing with relief. She walked outside, clutching the telegram in her hand. At last, she could go home! She paused outside and read the wire, more slowly this time, taking in her father's words.

Funds deposited at Bank of Bengal. Stop. Accessible immediately. Stop. Come home. Stop.

She seized Jamal's hand. 'I'm going home,' she said, her eyes shining.

Jamal's face fell. 'You are leaving India, memsahib?' He gave a sad smile. 'We will miss you, memsahib, but I am happy for you.'

'I must go to the bank now, Jamal,'

she told him. 'Will you please show me the way?'

The Bank of Bengal was an ornate red brick building and Grace felt quite intimidated as she passed through the doors into the echoing entrance hall. The air was hushed and there was a purposeful look to the men going about their business. She looked round, seeking a friendly face, noting that she was the only woman present.

A bank official approached and asked her business, looking askance when she told him her errand. Apparently they were not used to dealing with women and he asked why her husband had not accompanied her.

'My husband died recently,' she said.

At that she received another strange look and Grace guessed he was probably wondering why she wasn't in mourning. It wasn't any of his business, she thought. Anyway, she wasn't about to tell him she had no money for new clothes and that she was wearing her most sober outfit, having abandoned the yellow silk for a dress of dark blue with paler blue trimming.

The man muttered a word of apology and led her to a small alcove where they could talk privately. Firsly he wanted to see proof of her identity but she had none, excepting the telegram from her father.

'Is there no one in Calcutta who could vouch for you?' the man asked.

Grace shuddered at the thought of Mr Leeson, the only person she knew in this vast city, and she shook her head vehemently. There was Adam of course but she knew he had left the city to work on the wreck and she had no way of getting in touch with him.

After much hesitation the bank official finally accepted that she was entitled to the funds and helped her to open an account and transfer the money to it. She had no idea how much she would need for her passage home and she swallowed her pride and asked the man if he could help.

His manner thawed somewhat and he

said he would enquire at the shipping office for her. He then beckoned to a clerk and asked him to fetch some cash. 'This should be enough for you to be going on with,' he said, handing it to her. 'Don't hesitate to call if you need any help and I will let you know about booking your passage.'

As she shook his hand and left, she smiled. Despite his earlier caution, the bank official had been unable to resist an appeal for help from a young widow.

It was almost midday and far too hot to attempt the journey back to the bungalow just yet, although she now had sufficient funds to hire a vehicle. Deciding to have tiffin at the Imperial, she made her way there and gave Jamal a few coins, telling him to go and get himself some food and come back later. He grinned and scampered off, clutching the money in his hand.

She chose a table secluded by palms in huge ornate pots, hoping she would not be noticed, remembering being here with Adam and the awful way they had parted.

Was it only a week ago? He had not been out of her thoughts since that day and she wondered what he was doing now. She hoped that the dive was going well and tried not to think how dangerous the job was. He had told her that if they managed to salvage the whole cargo his share would make him a rich man. She prayed that he had been successful, mindful of the tragedy that had befallen his family and his longing to be able to do something to help his mother.

While she waited for her refreshments she walked over to a nearby table strewn with newspapers and magazines and picked up the Calcutta Courier. If she appeared to be reading no one would disturb her. Glancing at a small headline halfway down the page, she gasped in shock, and abruptly sat down at her table, almost tipping the chair over.

Diving tragedy on Hooghly River it read.

'Adam!' she gasped, clutching at her breast, and quickly scanning the short paragraph below the headline. There were no names — just the stark information that one of the English divers working on a shipwreck downriver had been trapped when the ship moved due to a sudden storm. Efforts had been made to revive him when he was brought up, but had not been successful. Another diver who had tried to rescue him was recovering in hospital.

She threw the paper down and leapt up, almost pushing the approaching waiter over in her haste. Outside she found Jamal sitting on the steps eating a chapatti. She grabbed his arm. 'The hospital, where is the hospital?' she shouted, shaking him when he answered in his own language.

She forced herself to stay calm and spoke more quietly. 'Jamal, I need to go to the hospital immediately,' she said. 'How do I get there?'

'Memsahib is hurt?' he asked, his voice puzzled.

She shook her head. 'A friend — I must see a friend,' she said, praying that Adam was only injured. He couldn't be dead, she told herself, not when they had just found each other! It didn't matter what had happened in the past or what the future might hold, she just wanted him to be all right.

'I will take you there, memsahib,' Jamal said, 'but it is a long way. I will fetch a cart.' He stepped into the road and gave a piercing whistle. Instead of the cumbersome bullock cart which Grace had been used to travelling in, a small two-wheeled carriage drawn by a pony pulled up. She climbed aboard and Jamal gave directions to the Indian driver.

★ ★ ★

At the hospital she asked Jamal and the driver to wait. Inside it was hot and noisy and Grace wrinkled her nose at the mingled smells of sickness and disinfectant. The walls of the corridor were lined with people waiting to be attended to while doctors and nurses hurried past, ignoring her pleas for assistance.

She walked down the corridor and, hearing a voice she recognised, entered a room off to the side. The Irish man she had met in Taylor's Emporium looked up and she knew she'd come to the right place. He came towards her and her heart sank at the grave look on his face.

'Mrs Eastwood? What are you doing here?' he asked.

Fear clutched her heart and she could hardly get the words out. 'Adam . . . ?' she whispered.

He stepped aside, gesturing to the bed in the corner of the room. 'There he is.'

Adam's eyes were closed and his face was parchment white. His bandaged hands lay outside the counterpane. He was so still that Grace could not bear to look.

As she took a hesitant step towards

the bed, his eyes opened, clouded with confusion. 'Grace?' he whispered. 'Is it really you . . . ?'

Tears welled up and she threw herself down beside the bed, running her hands through his hair, tracing the outline of his dear face. He sighed and his eyes closed again.

Grace turned to Adam's friend. 'What happened? Is he going to be all right?'

Mick nodded. 'He needs to rest, but yes, he'll recover. He stayed down too long.' He coughed. 'If it wasn't for Adam, I wouldn't be here now . . .'

'I don't understand,' Grace said. 'The paper said someone died. I thought . . .'

'That was Joe. I was trapped and Adam was trying to get me free. Joe tried to help but just as he moved the chest that had fallen on me, the wreck shifted again. Everything tumbled down on top of him. Adam pulled me out and I got to the surface all right.' He shook his head. 'Adam insisted on staying behind to look for Joe, but he couldn't find him. We hauled him up just in time. The other divers are still there, trying to find Joe's body.'

Grace uttered a little sob as the miracle of Adam's escape dawned on her. How like him to try and help others at such risk to himself, she thought.

She leaned over the bed and kissed his forehead, willing him to open his eyes again.

The doctor and Mick tried to persuade her to get some rest, but Grace insisted on staying and she had been at the hospital several hours before she remembered that Jamal was waiting for her, so she asked Mick to find him and send him home.

★ ★ ★

Adam remained semi-conscious for several days and Grace never left his side. She sat in a chair by the bed, holding his bandaged hand and talking softly, reminding him of their happy times, before the bitterness and enmity between their families had forced them apart.

She dozed fitfully from time to time. It was almost dawn and she had fallen asleep, no longer able to keep her eyes open, when she heard his voice.

She sat up quickly and leaned over the bed, searching his face, her heart thumping. She recalled that Thomas had been lucid immediately before his death and for a dreadful moment she feared that it was happening again, but Adam's eyes were clear and he was smiling.

'Gracie, my sweet Gracie,' he murmured through parched lips. 'I thought I was dreaming.'

'No, I'm really here,' she said. She held a cup to his lips and urged him to drink, then helped him to sit up.

'And I didn't dream that your husband . . . ?'

Grace shook her head. 'You didn't dream it. I'm a free woman now.' She felt no guilt at the relief she felt at no longer being bound to Thomas — he had treated her badly.

She waited breathlessly for Adam's reply. Would he be bound by honour and convention to refrain from saying what she longed to hear? She would have to make the first move.

As she opened her mouth to speak, he took her hand, wincing at the pain. 'This is probably the wrong time to say this, my love, but I want us to be married,' he said. 'Of course, we must wait a while . . . '

'Why wait?' she asked impulsively.

'But, your parents, Grace . . . I must ask their permission.'

'No, Adam,' Grace said firmly. 'I can choose for myself this time — and I choose you.'

His answering smile was a little sad. 'Gracie, my love. Are you sure? I know the bad feeling between our parents kept us apart and I can't deny I felt bitter about it. I blamed your father and James for years, but I realise now it was wrong of me. Do you think we can forget the past and start again?'

'All that doesn't matter now. We love each other, and that's all that matters.'

'Well, at least your brother can't object because I'm a poor fisherman. I can give you everything that Thomas did.'

'You can give me so much more,' Grace said. 'Your love is far more precious than all the jewels in the world.'

'Do you really mean that?' he asked.

Instead of answering she leaned over and kissed his cheek. His arms came round her and his lips sought hers. It was a little awkward with his still bandaged hands but he held her close, raining kisses on her eyes, her cheeks, her lips . . .

Grace responded ardently, remembering the first time he had kissed her properly — so long ago — but this was better than anything she had dreamed of. All the guilt she had felt for marrying a man she did not love, faded away and she kissed Adam again, savouring the moment and thrilling with the wonderful anticipation of the future that was yet to come.

THE END

We do hope that you have enjoyed reading this large print book.

Did you know that all of our titles are available for purchase?

We publish a wide range of high quality large print books including:
Romances, Mysteries, Classics
General Fiction
Non Fiction and Westerns

Special interest titles available in large print are:
The Little Oxford Dictionary
Music Book, Song Book
Hymn Book, Service Book

Also available from us courtesy of Oxford University Press:
Young Readers' Dictionary
(large print edition)
Young Readers' Thesaurus
(large print edition)

For further information or a free brochure, please contact us at:
Ulverscroft Large Print Books Ltd.,
The Green, Bradgate Road, Anstey,
Leicester, LE7 7FU, England.
Tel: (00 44) 0116 236 4325
Fax: (00 44) 0116 234 0205

Other titles in the
Linford Romance Library:

DESTINY CALLING

Chrissie Loveday

It is 1952. William Cobridge has returned from a trip to America a different man. Used to a life of luxury, he had been sent away to learn about life in the real world. He meets teacher Paula Frost on a visit to see her aunt, the housekeeper at Cobridge House. He is keen to see Paula again and asks her for a date. Could this be the start of a new romance? But then, things never go smoothly . . .

WHERE I BELONG

Helen Taylor

When a mysterious Italian man arrives on the doorstep in a storm, Maria can hardly turn him away, even though the guesthouse is closed for the winter. Maria's gentle care helps Dino recover from his distressing news, and soon she risks losing her heart to this charismatic stranger. But he has commitments that will take him far away, and her future is at the guesthouse. Can two people from different walks of life find a way to be together?

WED FOR A WAGER

Fenella Miller

Grace Hadley must enter into a marriage of convenience with handsome young Rupert Shalford, otherwise Sir John, her step-father, will sell her to the highest bidder. But Rupert's older brother Lord Ralph Shalford has other ideas and is determined he will have the union dissolved. However, Sir John is equally determined to recover his now missing step-daughter. Will Grace ever find the happiness she deserves?